CW00815791

HARP_ _

AT THE WATER'S EDGE

Copyright © 2014 by Harper Bliss
Edited by Cheyenne Blue
Cover design by Caroline Manchoulas
Published by Ladylit Publishing – a division of Q.P.S. Projects Limited - Hong Kong
ISBN-13 978-988-13637-6-3

For everyone who's been there

1

Driving past the yellow sign for West Waters instantly takes me back to a time when I was happy. It's not so much a single concrete memory as a tangled-up rush of them flooding my brain. My sister and I running barefoot in the grass around our cabin, dipping that first toe into the water on a carefree Saturday morning, bright-colored candy from the improvised shop by reception, the intoxicating smell of suntan lotion, Dad wearing the same pair of faded beige shorts for the entire weekend.

I pull into the parking lot and find a space close to the entrance. Even though the middle of August should be the peak of the vacation season, I count only two other cars in the lot. Everything looks satisfyingly familiar: the grassy curb, more neatly trimmed than I remember, the cabin roofs dotted against the mass of green surrounding the lake, a strip of water flickering under the midday sun in the distance. Yet as if belonging to another lifetime.

When I deposit my city-girl case on the uneven concrete, I realize I'll look like a fool if I try to roll it down the rickety path to reception. I grab the handle and lift the case, which is not very heavy. I only brought a few sets of clothes. Some books and a laptop—not for work, only for self-improvement. And only one blazer.

There's something about the air in this place. It takes me back to a simpler time, a time when it was a given that air was clean and pure, a time when I didn't worry so much. It's only a short walk to the wooden shack where I need to pick up the key. Through my parents, I know that both Mr. and Mrs. Brody are no longer with us, and that Kay is running things now.

I see her before she realizes I'm there. Crouched down, studying something on the ground, poking her finger into the soil. I clear my throat to announce my arrival.

I watch Kay shoot up, rubbing her hands on her shorts. "Hey." Her eyes light up when she recognizes me. "Well, I'll be damned. Little Ella Goodman."

Growing up, I was always shorter than the other kids my age. Now, I stand just as tall as Kay, whose build is stocky and muscular.

"Mom should have notified you that our cabin will be occupied—" I stop mid-sentence. Unable to shake the sensation that, somehow, she knows. That the reason I came here is plastered across my face.

Kay tilts her head, regarding me with some sort of glint of expectation in her eyes. Of course, she doesn't know. Hardly anyone does.

"Yep. Dee warned me." Her voice is matter-of-fact, with the delivery of someone who never questions her self-confidence. "Let's go in."

I follow her inside the shack—or 'the shop' as my family called it when I came here as a child. From the outside, I hadn't noticed the extension to the side.

"I spruced it up a bit." Kay must have noticed the look

of surprise on my face. "We even have a laundromat in the back these days."

"Fancy." I scan the neat aisles, all pleasantly lit and shiny, and what looks like a brand new fridge and freezer against the back wall.

"It isn't the eighties anymore, Ella. We have Wi-Fi now." Kay leans against a proper reception desk—laptop and all—and grins at me. "Let me get your key… card." She taps a few times on the laptop's keyboard, opens a drawer and produces a key card like in a hotel. "Have you liked our Facebook page?" she asks, a grin slipping across her face as she hands me the card.

"I will," I stammer.

"Don't worry, it's not mandatory, but a check-in on Facebook is always appreciated." She leans her elbows on the counter. "Unless you're here on the down-low, of course."

I don't immediately know what to say, so unprepared am I by seeing Kay—whom I haven't seen since I last visited West Waters many years ago—so quickly after arriving and the unexpected topic of conversation that's making me feel uncomfortable.

"I'm just screwing with you." She rests her almond-shaped eyes on me—again, that sensation that she is looking right through me and seeing all my scars. "Welcome to West Waters. I hope you enjoy your stay with us. It can get quite busy over the weekends, but you should be fine out there in the Goodman cabin. You should see what they've done to the place."

I vaguely remember my mother mentioning remodeling the cabin a few years ago, but I was probably too busy to take in the details. Listening to her with one ear, while scheduling a lecture in New York and going over a research report.

"Can't wait." I flip the key card between my fingers a few times, desperate to make more small talk—not because I'm so eager but because it's what expected in a situation like this. "Is it just you running the place?"

Kay shrugs. "Most cabins are privately owned, so not too much fuss for me."

"What about the off season?" The next question comes easily because I'm genuinely interested in the answer.

"People come even when it rains. It's only in the depths of winter that it goes really quiet. Then I take the time to think of ways of improving West Waters, usually over a few beers at The Attic." Her chuckle comes from a deep place, like an old man's laugh.

A bell that I hadn't even noticed when I followed Kay in, goes off, as a man with wild white hair walks in. He tilts his chin when he spots me and, out of nowhere, winks at me.

"Uncle Pete," Kay says in a loud, booming voice. "Here's your reading material for today."

As the man shuffles to the counter I make my way to the door. Kay presents him with *The New York Times* and *The Northville Gazette*.

"See you later, Ella," she shouts.

I give her a quick wave and exit the shop. Once outside, I need to scan my surroundings to orientate myself. My family's cabin is situated on the edge of the grounds, near the most western tip of the lake. I breathe in a large gulp of air, then another, enjoying the quiet, sun-drenched hum of a summer afternoon in Northville, Oregon.

————

Kay was right. From the outside, our cabin looks the same, but the inside could easily appear in *Country Living*, the 'maximizing a tiny space in a semi-fashionable way edition'. The wooden boards lining the walls and ceilings are new and light-brown, giving the interior a shiny, but cozy feel.

The kitchenette—taking up half of the lounge area—boasts new appliances, but the true stunner is the bathroom. A dark-gray tiled walk-in shower, flanked by one of those modern water basins, the kind of which you can never be sure where the water comes from.

I remember an unanswered email from my mother containing pictures of this overhaul. If it weren't for that, I'd be suspicious that, somehow, they did this all for me.

The second bedroom, too narrow for more furniture, still houses bunk-beds, but the old closet has been replaced by a built-in one, made with the same planks as the rest of the cabin.

I stopped joining my parents for weekends here as soon as they allowed me to stay home with Nina. She was seventeen—and up to no good—and I was fourteen, and already so at odds with the world. Today, I deposit my suitcase in the room where my parents always slept, and even though it doesn't feel quite right, I don't particularly feel like crashing on the bottom bunk in the room next door. For all the times I came here as a child, I never once slept in the master bedroom.

More than anything, I'm drawn to the lake. I kick off the sneakers I wore for driving and head to the porch running around both sides and rear of the cabin. From there, it's easy to reach the landing that leads directly to the lake. I sit and let my feet dangle in the water, instantly transported back to the hours I spent here as a child. Observing the water creatures, watching the sun climb until it was almost perfectly on top of the lake, making the surface glimmer like a mirror broken in all the right places, waiting until it dipped behind the trees on the other side, in the early dusk of summer, and painted the lake orange.

Judging from where the sun now hangs in the clear blue sky, already having started its descent, I figure it must be around four. A beer would be nice. I'm sure I can pick some up in the shop, and some snacks that will have to do for dinner tonight.

———

Later, when the sun has completely disappeared behind the dense tree tops, and I sit overlooking the water with a cold beer in my hand, a rustling to the left of the porch startles me. I'm so used to city noises—a constant buzz of traffic, road works, and endless construction—that now, when all around me an unfamiliar sort of quiet reigns, I start at the slightest ripple of sound.

"Hey." Kay materializes in front of me. "Didn't mean to give you a fright." She sports that smile again, the one that indicates a friendly but don't-mess-with-me attitude. In high school, she was three years above me, leaving us in decidedly different social circles. But I saw her around at West Waters sometimes, running on the sandy track on the other side of the lake, or—a more distant memory—just once, canoodling with Jim Straw behind a tree only a few feet away from our cabin. "You left this in the shop." She holds up my wallet. "Figured you might want it back."

"Oh, shoot." I hadn't even noticed it was missing. "Thank you so much." She climbs the two porch stairs and holds it out to me. Gratefully, I pocket it. "The least I can do is offer you a beer." It's my first night here and I'm not really in the mood for small talk, but politeness always wins.

"I won't say no to that." She winks and parks her behind unceremoniously in the wicker chair next to mine. "How's that sister of yours doing?"

She doesn't waste any time asking the hard questions. I grab her a beer from the cool box next to my chair and offer it to her, avoiding her piercing glance.

"Dee and John never really mention her when they come here, you know? While they can't shut up about Little Ella, fancy professor at Boston U. What is it again? Chemistry?"

"Biology," I'm quick to correct. "Plant and microbial ecosystem ecology, to be precise."

"Damn, sounds complicated." Kay brings the bottle to her lips and drops her head back. "Is that why you came here? To study our shrubbery?" She gives that deep, rumbling laugh again.

I shake my head. "I've taken a leave of absence."

"Sounds like a fussy name for a vacation to me." With a few quick draughts, Kay empties half her bottle. "So how about Nina? Where is she hanging out these days."

"Last I heard, she was in New Zealand, but we're not really in touch that much."

Kay nods as if she understands, as if my evasive answer is more than enough explanation. She drains the last of her beer and plants the bottle on the wooden table in front of her. "I'll leave you in peace. Thanks for the beverage." She rises with unexpected elegance. "You know the drill, right? Dial 911 for emergencies." She grins. "If you were to need me personally, I'm still in the lodge behind the shop." She gives me a quick nod of the head. "Night, night, Little Ella." The last I see of her face, before she spins on her heel and leaves, is a crooked smirk.

2

The next morning over breakfast—a muesli bar bought at the shop—I gaze out over the water again. The stillness helps with the exercises Dr. Hakim taught me to clear my mind of 'everything that doesn't belong'. But it's hard to block out the impending visit to my parents' house. The place where I grew up. The place where I learned to express my frustration through deadly, stone-cold silence. I learned from the best: my mother.

A ripple catches in the water, cracking the surface. It's only seven a.m. but perhaps Uncle Pete likes an early morning swim. Regular splashing sounds approach the landing. It's so quiet, I can hear rhythmic intakes of breath as Kay swims through my field of vision with strong freestyle strokes. After reaching the edge of the lake, she stops briefly, her eyes barely peeking over the surface of the water.

Physical exercise will help, Dr. Hakim said numerous times. I estimate I could possibly make it to the other, shorter end of the lake without too much difficulty.

"Early bird?" Kay shouts at me from the water, her voice shattering the calmness of the morning.

In response, I shrug and slant my head. I've been awake for hours, but, like a good girl, I tried to stay in bed as long as I could possibly stand it.

Kay tilts her chin and ducks back under, swimming back to her side of the lake—although, I guess every side of the lake is hers.

———

My mother opens her arms to greet me, as though she has suddenly turned into a person who displays her love through hugging. The embrace is awkward—all stiff limbs and not knowing what to say. My father keeps his distance, just plants an almost-air kiss on my cheek.

"Have you settled in well?" my mother asks. "Do you like the new decor?" In my head, I hear: *Is it really so much better than staying here with us?*

"It's wonderful." I haven't set foot in my parents' living room for years. Always too busy to book a flight. Always finding the perfect excuse not to make the trip.

"How's the rental?" Dad looks out of the window to the driveway. "You could have used the—"

"I know, Dad. It's fine, really." I'm already staying in their cabin and the last thing I want is to feel as though I owe them anything for using objects that belong to them.

"Coffee?" Mom asks. Their initial invitation was for lunch, but I couldn't bear the thought of having to sit through a meal with them. I'm not ready for that just yet.

"Black, please." Perhaps it's strange that my own mother doesn't know how I take my coffee.

"She drinks more than she eats these days," Dad says as he takes a seat at the kitchen table, not offering any more explanation. He looks like a man who drinks just as much as he eats himself.

Already, I can't stop myself from glancing at the clock—the same one they've had for decades, with such a deep, loud tick-tock that sometimes, when I was upstairs in my room and the house was quiet, I could have sworn I could hear it all the way through the ceiling.

When Mom deposits the cups and an apple cake on the table, I notice how bony her arms have become—and I know it's because of me. If not politeness, then at least guilt will keep me here for the next few hours.

"Are you not having any?" I ask her after she has served me and Dad.

"I'm sure your father will have my share." With that, the topic of conversation is firmly closed. My Dad emits a barely audible sigh at her well-worn remark.

I'm not particularly hungry myself, my stomach having tightened the instant I pulled up in the driveway, but I eat the piece of cake anyway, lest they think I suffer from a lack of appetite—and all the associations they could make in their minds.

"Are you feeling better?" Mom asks after the silence has stretched into minutes, only interrupted by the clinking sounds of our forks against the plates, and, apparently, has become unbearable even for her.

"Much." And I know I should say more, but the words don't come. I suppose that the reason why my family is so bad at starting conversations is because we're so skilled at killing them.

Think happy thoughts, I tell myself. I didn't get that nugget of wisdom from Dr. Hakim, I read it on the internet. On one of those wellness websites that endlessly recycles the same articles. So, I think of West Waters, of the stillness of the lake this morning, because honestly, I don't have that much else to think of in that department.

"What will you do with your time?" Dad asks. "Wouldn't it be better to stay occupied?"

I asked myself that same question over and over again before deciding to come here. But work was part of the problem. How I completely buried myself in it. Took on more seats on more committees than any member of faculty— despite finding committee work the biggest waste of time ever invented. But anything was good enough to keep me from going home to my house and the blackness that awaited me there.

"I'm sure she knows best, John," my mother comes to my defense, and it strangely touches me—tears at the ready behind my eyes and everything. But she's wrong, because if I had truly known better, I wouldn't have done what I did.

"I won't be teaching the first term," I state, as though I'm facing a class of students instead of my parents. "I'm only slated to return in the New Year."

Then, out of nowhere, my mother's hand lands on my wrist. I flinch because I hadn't expected it, but it only makes her claw her fingers deeper into my flesh. "If there's anything—" she starts to say, but chokes up.

I swallow the tightness out of my throat—images of the splendor of West Waters flooding my brain—and put my hand on hers. It's all I've got for now.

"I—uh, I'd like to get a picture from my old room," I stammer, uncomfortable in the moment as it drags on.

"Sure." Mom removes her hand and stares into her empty coffee cup.

"You still know the way, I hope," Dad says in an overly cheerful voice that doesn't fit the mood at all.

"Sure." I push my chair back, my eyes fixed on the stair-well, and I can't get out of there fast enough.

Once upstairs, the bedroom where I spent my youth is still semi-intact. The bed I slept in is still there, but numerous other objects have found their way in. Toaster ovens Dad has won at card games, old electrical appliances Mom can't bear to throw out, a worn, deflated lilo we used to take to West Waters.

The picture I'm looking for is one of Nina and me, taken outside the cabin. I find it face-down on the corner of my former desk. Nina's at least two heads taller than me, her hair straw-blond and scraggly—and always that glint of trouble in her eyes. She must be ten, still young enough to wrap an arm around my shoulders for a picture, and I'm seven. I am smiling broadly, one tooth missing, my hair much darker than my sister's, and, despite the toothless grin, my glance much more demure.

I look around the room but the anticipated wave of nostalgia doesn't come. Too much time has passed, too many new memories have erased the ones I made here. I wonder what Nina's old room looks like these days, but instead of walking across the landing to find out, I take the stairs down, and hide the picture in my purse.

"We're having Aunt Mary over for dinner this weekend," Mom says when I re-enter the living room. "Will you co—"

"Don't pressure her, Dee," Dad cuts her off.

"It's fine," I quickly jump in to avoid further arguing about me. "I'll come, but I should go now. I want to get to the store before it closes."

Their goodbye is casual and quick—the goodbye to someone they'll see again soon. This time it's true, despite it being the exact same type of farewell we always exchange.

———

Back at West Waters, the sun is already bleeding out its last rays of the day over the lake, and it all weighs heavy on me again. Before putting the groceries away, I lean against the kitchen counter and dig up the picture I snatched from my childhood bedroom.

You were always the easy one. I hear my mother's voice in my head. *You never caused us trouble like your sister did.* Dr. Hakim has taught me that there is absolutely no use in trying to guess what someone else might be thinking. I used to sit in his office three times a week, motionless, detached, and impossible to read. I'd listen to his baritone full of wisdom, stare at the liver spots on his hands as he rubbed a finger over his thin beard. It reminded me of a social communications class I took in college.

Our teacher Mrs. Kissinger, on whom I had a raging, silent crush, filmed us while we talked about ourselves for a few minutes. When she went over the videos in class, teaching us about body language and what it revealed about a person, she basically skipped my segment, stating that, in all her years of conducting this experiment, she'd never come across someone as non-verbally uncommunicative, the way I sat stock-still, my hands slipped safely underneath my thighs.

Nobody ever noticed.

A whistling sound outside shakes me out of my reverie, followed by Kay's deep voice. "Knock, knock."

I step outside to find her on my porch, moist hair drawn into a tight ponytail.

"Tonight's my weekly drinking night at The Attic. I was wondering if you felt like tagging along. Reconnect with some folks from way back when." She's wearing dungarees, split low at the sides, over nothing more than a tank top.

Flummoxed, I push a strand of hair behind my ear. "Thanks, but not tonight." *Or ever.*

"Are you sure, Little Ella? You look as if you could do with letting your hair down a bit."

I give her a well-practiced smile. The exact same one I

used for years on everyone I knew. It even works on myself sometimes. "Maybe next week," I lie. "Still settling in and all that."

A scrunch of the lips and a dip of the head, and she's gone, her hands tucked deep in the front pockets of her dungarees, like a farmer leaving his field after a good day.

3

The rain starts coming down hard around three in the morning. Loud pelts—like stones being thrown at high speed—coming down without mercy on the wooden roof above me. Having lain awake through many a rain storm in my youth, I know this one, just like any bout of summer rain, will pass by morning, leaving the lake and its surroundings aglow in a new, lighter clarity at dawn. Nevertheless, any hope of sleep soon escapes me. Which is fine, because I have all of the next day to do nothing.

Have you considered that, on top of everything else, you might be suffering from burn-out? Dr. Hakim asked in our first session. I thought he looked smart in a well-worn way. Brown tweed jacket with patches over the elbows. Intelligent, dark eyes behind rimless glasses. One slim leg slung over the other.

Doing nothing is the cure. Accepting emptiness. Learning to exist in the quietness between bursts of activity. It's harder in the dark of night, nothing or no one around but memories I'm trying to erase. Out of nowhere, a shot of worry makes its way through me. I hope Kay made it back safely from the bar, before the rain came. She doesn't strike me as the type to be foolish enough to drive after too many beers—but really, I have no way of knowing.

I grab my phone from the night stand and touch it so it lights up, more for illumination than anything else. I hold it in front of me and make my way to the kitchen, where I pick up a glass of water, before heading to the porch.

Clouds cover the moon, and the darkness, pierced by rapid, splashing sounds, is almost complete around me, making the screen of my phone glow brighter. Automatically, my thumb goes to the e-mail application, but I removed all work-related accounts before I left Boston. I only have one personal account installed on it, but there are no new e-mails since I last checked before going to bed.

To kill time, I go on Facebook and search for West Waters. A small smile tugs at my lips as I click 'like' on the page. I scroll through a few comments Kay has left in response to other people's, and click on her profile. My thumb hovers over the 'Add Friend' button. *Why not?* As always, my brain comes up with many reasons not to, but I'm curious to see what hides behind the privacy settings Kay has enforced. A flick of the thumb is all it takes. *Friend request sent.*

Two seconds later, the red circle indicating a notification lights up at the top of my screen. *Friend request accepted.* I guess I'm not the only one who can't sleep through the rain. I barely have a chance to check out her profile before I get a private message. I don't know why, but my heart beats a little faster as I start reading it.

Still awake, Little Ella?

. . .

Instead of typing what I want to—*Please, stop calling me that*—I ask if she made it home safely.

I always do. Best get some sleep now. My day starts early.

Good night, I type back and click on her name. Her profile picture is one of just her head sticking out of the lake, eyes squinting against the sun, white teeth glinting in between curled up lips. Her relationship status says: *It's complicated*. I can't help but snicker. Kay seems like the most uncomplicated woman I've ever met, but I guess looks can be deceiving. Perhaps it's a joke, or, for her, complicated means long-distance or something. I've only been here a day, but I haven't noticed any signs of someone living with her in the lodge behind the shop.

And what do I care anyway?

The rain is easing on the surface of the lake. I decide to go back to bed and try to catch a few more hours of sleep. Not easy when medication is no longer allowed.

––––––

"Best enjoy the last few hours of quiet."

I instantly recognize Kay's gravelly voice. I open my eyes and stare into her smile.

"The weekend crowd will be arriving soon. It's the last big one of the summer. After that, things should die down." She chuckles. "I'm only informing you because you seem like someone who values her privacy."

I push myself up a bit on my lounge chair, relieved I'm not wearing my bikini as I had initially planned, but shorts that reach the middle of my thighs and a halter top. Not that it makes my skin look any less milky white. Still, I feel less exposed this way.

"Oh shoot." She crouches until her eyes are level with mine. "I didn't wake you, did I?"

"No, just trying to absorb some vitamin D." I feel Kay's gaze glide across my body.

"You're probably too smart to forget, Professor, but I hope you applied sun screen."

Was that a crack at the impossible paleness of my legs and arms? "SPF 50," I say. "I'm hoping to go lower soon." My top clings to my skin in the small of my back because of the sweat that has pooled there. "Full house this weekend?"

"Pretty much." She looks over the lake, momentarily lost in thought. Her skin has the same tone as Dr. Hakim's brown tweed jacket. I woke up to an e-mail from him this morning, phrased in the same unobtrusive way he used to treat me.

I hope you're doing well, Ella. Call me any time.

"We're having a bonfire on Sunday night. Just sayin'. Not invitin'. Everyone's welcome." A sassiness has seeped into her voice, giving it a higher pitch.

"I'll keep that in mind."

She shoots me one of what I've already come to think of as her trademark winks before pushing herself up. "I'll leave you to it. The water's wonderful today, by the way."

I watch her walk away. Her navy shorts barely cover her ass as she saunters away from the patch of lawn in front of our cabin. I recline back in my chair and ponder Dr. Hakim's e-mail. *Am I doing well?* I certainly don't feel the need to call him. I guess I'm doing as well as can be expected.

———

The days at West Waters are slow, so I'm actually quite happy to have the distraction of dinner with my parents and Aunt Mary on Saturday evening.

She grips me in a tight bear hug the instant she sees me. "Oh, Ella. Oh, Ella," she keeps repeating. Aunt Mary is like a more filled-out, taller version of my mother. A quick-mouthed high school teacher who was promoted to principal the last fifteen years of her career. Unlike my mother, she likes to say things out loud. Not this, though. There are some things that no one wants to speak of out loud.

Aunt Mary has four highly successful children of her own, and all but one live close by. Between them, they've already given her seven grandchildren, with an eighth on the way. It's only natural for her to talk about her offspring in a light tone, laughter in her voice, pride glittering in her eyes. As she does, it's as if I can see a sheen of bitterness coat itself around my mother's skin. It's not as much envy, I think, as the loss of something she never even experienced. Something that could potentially brighten up her days.

And I know it's not my fault—Dr. Hakim and I have covered this extensively—but the guilt still nags at me. It's there, showing up faithfully, every time I walk into this house.

Every time Aunt Mary wants to ask me a question, she bites it back, her mouth opening and closing like a fish gulping for air on dry land. Just like everyone else who knows, she's unsure of what is safe ground. What is allowed to be asked, to be said. Soon, the conversation dies a predictable, natural death.

But it's not the silence that falls around us that makes me freeze up. It's the un-spokenness of it all, of 'the thing' that hangs above all of our heads. The precise reason why I've come. But I've only just arrived and I'm nowhere near ready.

Then, just as the tension becomes unbearable, Aunt Mary hammers the final nail into Mom's coffin.

"Any news from Nina?" It's not malice, I'm sure of that. It's not exactly an innocent question either, more a desperate conversation starter.

"She's in New Zealand. She was an extra in *The Hobbit*," I'm quick to say, to give my mother time to regroup. Nina e-mailed me this nugget of news months ago, and I scoured the IMDb to verify her claim, but the list of extras was so long, I couldn't find her in it.

"The what?" Aunt Mary asks.

"It's a big movie franchise. A spin off of *Lord of the Rings*," Dad says.

"I see." Aunt Mary nods as if she's reflecting deeply on this. From the set of her jaw, I easily deduct this visit will end soon, for which I'm grateful.

When she leaves, she hugs me tightly again. Neither Mom's nor Dad's side of the family—and least of all our own—are naturally tactile people, and learning to accept a family member's arms around me is still so foreign that I find it hard to enjoy the offered comfort. Instead, I stand stiffly inside her embrace, my muscles automatically rejecting this sort of display of affection. But Aunt Mary's hug is different from Mom's, more matter-of-fact and less desperate. The quick, solid embrace of a woman who has gotten used to comforting grandchildren.

Only a few minutes after she's out the door, I'm quick to say my goodbyes as well. On the way back to West Waters, I drive past The Attic, keeping my eyes peeled for Kay's car. What does she do for entertainment in this town apart from having a beer with the same people every week?

By the time I drive up to what I've started to consider as *my* parking spot at West Waters, my head is overflowing with questions I'd like to ask Kay. To my dismay, one of the week-enders has parked in my spot, and I need to maneuver into another space. I can't wait for the weekend to be over and have the lake to myself again.

4

On Sunday night, I find my own surprise in attending the bonfire reflected in the expression on Kay's face when she spots me.

"You made it," she says, and slaps me on the shoulder. The temperatures have dropped and Kay has wrapped herself in a dark-gray fleece hoodie and pants. I guess there's not much use for decorum in a small town like Northville.

I wear the only blazer I packed—a reminder of my life in Boston, which, already, after only a few days here, where time seems to freeze, appears to belong to another lifetime. Or maybe I'm just eager to forget.

"Are you sure about that?" She scans my outfit with a scrutinizing glance. "You'll have to take that to the dry-cleaners after tonight."

First, I'm not sure what she's getting at, but when she points her thumb in the direction of the fire, I understand she's referring to the smell of smoke and ashes that will penetrate the fabric of my blazer.

"Oh, it's fine." I scan the people gathered around the fire, bottles of beers and plastic cups of wine in their hands, for familiar faces. In the pale-orange light of the flames, the only person I recognize is Uncle Pete.

"Here, take mine." Kay starts unzipping her hoodie, revealing a powder-blue v-neck t-shirt clinging to her chest. "I'll take your fancy jacket inside."

Our eyes meet and in the instant of hesitation that comes next, as if following a command, I slip out of my blazer and hand it to her.

While she saunters to the lodge behind the shop, I let the cozy fleece—warmed up by Kay's body heat—envelop me, and a faint whiff of her scent wafts up into my nostrils. It's not perfume, but an unexpectedly flowery soap, an unmistakable summer smell that takes me back to way before all of this began.

Silently, I look around me again, at these strangers with their children, their own stories safely tucked away behind the masks of their—mostly—carefree faces.

When Kay returns, in a navy sweater with the West Waters logo displayed on her chest, I know the warm glow that spreads through me at the sight of her isn't only due to the growing fire. But, this moment, too, will pass. This fleeting second of being at peace with things. It always does.

"Ella Goodman?" From behind me, a beer-drenched voice calls my name. "Is that you?"

I turn and stare straight into Drew Hester's pudgy, red-nosed, loose-skinned face. I remember my mother's glee when she found out I was dating one of the Hester boys. To this day, I'm still not sure if it was because Drew's father, Bruce, owned half of the land in Northville, or because, even at sixteen—quite some time before I worked up the nerve to tell her—Mom had her suspicions about me.

"Drew. Wow," I sputter.

Kay pushes a bottle of cold beer into my hand and I eagerly accept it, locking my eyes with hers for a moment.

"What brings you to these parts?" My teenage romance with Drew was short-lived, restricted to a few sloppy kisses and unsuccessful groping sessions behind the town hall.

"Family." I say it in the tone I use when one of my students is acting up during a Friday late afternoon class.

"Hey." He slants his long body in my direction, his beer breath slamming into my face. "Is it true what I hear? Is that why you dumped me all these years ago?" He narrows his eyes as though he just reached an important conclusion with the few remaining brain cells operating his mind. "Oh, I see." He looks at me, then turns his head to Kay, and back. "Oh, yes."

His bloodshot eyes rest on me. For all the battles I've fought with myself, my sexual identity has never been much of an issue. But the way he alludes to Kay's stuns me into silence nonetheless.

"That's enough, big guy." Kay steps in—literally blocking my body with hers.

"Didn't mean to offend." Drew holds up his hands. "Let's catch up before you leave, Ella." With a drunken man's swagger—ridiculous and wobbly—he turns and disappears into the darkness.

"Don't mind him. He doesn't get out much." Kay's voice is soothing and apologetic. "If and when he does," she shrugs, "well…"

But I don't care about Drew and his ignorant questions. I want to ask her, but don't immediately know how without coming across just as rude as Drew.

Surely I would have heard about it if Kay were a lesbian like me. After I came out, despite my mother's urging to keep 'my news' quiet—a wish I obeyed not because she wanted it that way, but because I wasn't exactly keen on becoming the talk of the town either—rumors started cropping up almost immediately. Halted whispers when I went into the butcher's.

Hushed voices at The Attic, not just one of Kay's favorite watering holes, but also my father's preferred spot for relaxation.

"It's fine," I say, instead, but the discomfort has settled. Not because of the brief, almost silly interaction with Drew, but because of the same old question that keeps rearing its head: was it really a good idea to come here?

Kay bumps her shoulder into mine. "They'll all be gone tomorrow. We'll have the place to ourselves all week."

I giggle and pull Kay's fleece tightly around my body, resisting the urge to lean into her.

"Kay." A vaguely familiar looking woman dressed in a linen pants suit walks up to us. Her grey hair is done up in a neat, tight bun. "That man in your shop says you've run out of diet coke, surely that can't be the case."

"I'm on it, Mrs. Innis. Come with me." After Kay has addressed her by name, I realize the woman taught me in third grade.

I stare into the fire while emptying the rest of the beer Kay gave me. She's fully engaged in chit-chat with Mrs. Innis and slowly, a circle of mostly elderly people forms around her, obstructing my view. I stand too far away to hear what she's saying and, growing tired of the shrieking children playing tag and nearly bumping into me a dozen times, I retreat back to the privacy of my cabin.

———

I've built my own fire in the pit between the porch and the lake and, because of the cracking sparks and light whoosh of the flames, I don't hear her footsteps as she approaches.

"Thought you might want this back." Kay stands next to me, holding my blazer.

I'm still wrapped in her sweater, drinking more beer.

"Thanks." I look up at her. "Want one?" I present my half-empty bottle.

She nods and sits on the edge of the porch.

While I duck inside to stow away my jacket and fetch Kay a beer, I believe I know why she has come. Or perhaps I've had one beer too many.

"Don't like crowds, huh?" Kay asks when I sit next to her, our feet dangling in the air, our thighs nearly touching.

"Depends." I let my gaze rest on the flickering orange glow in front of us. "Can I ask you something?"

A loud, gurgling chuckle erupts from Kay's mouth. "By all means, Little Ella. By all means."

I turn my head to look at her. Her lips are drawn into a thin smirk, eyes brimming in the light of the fire.

"Are you gay?"

A short silence before she replies. "No." She tilts her head a bit more. "Which doesn't mean I've never fallen in love with a woman."

"Oh." I feel my face flush. "I'm sorry. I didn't mean—"

"Don't worry your pretty little head about it."

The skin of my cheeks feels as though the flames have started licking it with broad, sweltering strokes across my face.

"So bloody ignorant," I murmur. "I should know better."

"I'm not that thin-skinned, and, living here, I'm used to worse."

"But still." I sip from my beer, hoping it will cool the flush on my cheeks.

"I'm truly not fussed with what people think about me. It's my life and I do what I do." Lightly, she jabs her elbow into my biceps. "You're not like that. I can tell."

I huff out some air. "Let's just say I'm a work in progress." My stomach tightens. I drink more beer.

"We all are."

"You look pretty much complete to me." My words come out as a whisper, disappearing instantly into the soft roar of the flames.

I don't expect the loud cackle. When I look at Kay she's shaking her head, an amused glint in her eyes.

"We all have our thing, Ella. All have our very own cross to bear."

I wish I was the kind of person who could sit on the edge of that porch with Kay until the morning, continuing this line of conversation, but already I feel myself clamming up —my tongue and thoughts growing paralyzed.

Kay drains the rest of her beer with quick, quiet gulps. "Permission to go inside and get us another?"

"Yes." I nod almost feverishly, before my anxious brain can take over and ruin everything.

When she returns, I watch her sit gracefully, her movements supported by strong muscles.

"To a quiet September," she says as she clinks the neck of her bottle against mine.

In the silence that ensues I imagine telling her; I imagine her probing, kind eyes on me as I do.

"When Dee informed me about the occupancy of your family's cabin she didn't give a check-out date."

It takes a few seconds before my brain registers her statement as a question. "Yeah, uh, no. I'm not sure yet when I'll be leaving."

"Rekindling your love affair with Northville?"

"Something like that." I suck in a deep breath. "Bit of a burn-out situation in Boston. Buried myself in work a tad too much."

"You could have gone to Hawaii, though. Or to Europe. Some place a bit more exotic than this sleepy old town." Her voice is low, nonjudgmental, barely quizzing—just conversational.

"Sometimes, you need to go back to where you came from."

"Not so easy for me." She gives a light chuckle. "I was born and bred at this lake, and I'm still here."

"Have you never felt the urge to leave?" I try to keep my tone level.

She shrugs. "Not really. This is what I know. I feel good here." A wide, swooping gesture of her hand. "Look at this. Why would I want to leave this behind?"

Instead of letting my gaze drift across the lake, its surface glowing in the light of the flames, I stare at Kay's hand: long fingers, trimmed nails, no rings.

"But what do you do for, uh, entertainment?"

"Entertainment?" The word rolls off her tongue like the punchline to a bad joke. "Can you be more specific?"

The blush that left me earlier is back. "Movies? Museums? Culture in general, I guess."

"When I have a crushing, burning desire to see a painting or some wacko modern art installation I probably wouldn't understand, I take my car and drive to the city." An edge has crept into her voice—as if she has had to answer a question like this too many times in her life. "And when was the last time you saw a good movie in the theatre? A movie which you can truly say was worth paying twenty bucks for?"

"I'm sorry. I didn't mean to imply—"

"That small town people have boring lives?" The friendliness is back in her voice, a smile breaking on her lips again. "Most people I know here, I've known all my life. That's a strong connection. And trust me, they provide all the *entertainment* I need."

Perhaps I should be jealous of Kay's ties to Northville's community—of the feelings of safety, of truly being known —that come with life-long acquaintance. But, apart from a few, very brittle, family ones, I have no ties here. Only nostalgia and a deep, deep melancholy that I know has sprouted here, that is rooted in the soil of this very town.

"My turn to ask a question." Kay swings her ankle into mine. I'll need some more time to adjust to her questions-disguised-as-statements way of conducting a conversation.

"Sure." The beer has made me light-headed now, almost carefree.

"Will it just be you in the cabin all this time? Or will a lady from the oh-so exciting city be joining you at some point?"

Thank goodness the alcohol is helping me to relax enough that I don't blush at her question. "No, just me," I say in a small voice. *I'm very good at chasing city ladies out of my life.* I don't say the last part out loud.

"What? A hot shot Boston U professor like you is single? Just when I thought all was right with the world."

"I have a PhD in Biology. It's not the most sexy subject."

"Could have fooled me." For the first time, Kay's flow of words is interrupted by something, perhaps self-conscious-ness, or maybe the beer is getting to her as well. "I mean, with the birds and the bees and all."

I laugh at this—a raw, deep chuckle that's been waiting to come out. A release of tension. "What was your major in college?"

"College?" Kay bangs her beer bottle onto the deck. "This is where I went to college, learned everything I ever needed to know." That sweeping gesture of her arm again—my eyes once again drawn to her hand. "I'd better get going. Lots of check-outs in the morning."

"I'm sorry—"

"You should really learn to stop apologizing for every little thing you say, Ella. Trust me, the world will survive without you being constantly sorry for everything."

Taken aback, I have no reply—just a familiar crushing feeling in my gut. Stomach dropping, chest tightening.

"Good night." Kay touches me lightly on the arm before taking the two stairs down off the deck and disappearing into the darkness.

5

The next day when I emerge from the cabin around noon—head fuzzy, stomach upset—the sun hangs high in the sky, bathing West Waters in the light I remember from my youth. But I'm no longer ten years old. I'm forty and a mess.

When I walk back inside to check the fridge and find it near-empty, I consider my options. For some reason—always the same one—I can't bear the thought of bright super-market lights, so I decide to take a load of laundry to the shop at reception and pick up some unhealthy snacks while I'm there. I also want to apologize to Kay… until I remember her parting words from last night. But still, I want to express at least a little bit of regret over my baffling igno-rance when it comes to her.

Unwashed—I'll have a swim and a shower later—I trudge down the path to reception, having forgotten that most of the weekenders are checking out today, leaving their keys with Kay, and scheduling cleanings and such. I'm still a few yards away when the unbearable sound of too much high-pitched laughter makes me stop in my tracks. But it's just a family of five making their way from the shack to the parking lot. Two small girls are skipping from one tile to the other—the exact same thing my sister and I used to do when leaving West Waters.

In the moment during which I'm trying to decide whether to turn back or go ahead, Kay appears in the doorway of the shop. Instantly, a wave of comfort washes over me, her consistent presence already forming a safety net I will have no choice but to reject.

"Morning," she shouts, a sly grin on her lips.

I re-sling my laundry bag over my shoulder and head in her direction.

"You don't have to wash that." Her eyes spot the sweater she loaned me last night at the top of my overflowing laundry bag. "Have you eaten?"

I shake my head, suddenly self-conscious because of not washing. "I'll grab some—"

"Breakfast bars? Nuh-uh. I'm not having it. Put your laundry in and meet me back here. I'll cook you some eggs Brody-style."

"But—" I try to protest but I already know resistance is futile.

Today, she's wearing olive green shorts and a faded black t-shirt. Her skin gleams in the midday sunlight. Hands on her hips, she tilts her head and it's enough to make me shut up.

"Go on." She moves out of the entrance to let me through and I saunter to the back of the shop where I figure out how the washer works and set it in motion.

When I arrive back at reception, she's busy with Uncle Pete, handing him his newspapers. He turns to the door and offers me a sweet smile that, instantly, warms me to the core.

Kay guides me to the lodge-like bungalow behind reception. "Please have a seat out here and give me a shout when someone approaches the shop. They should all have gone, but it's not uncommon on the day after the bonfire for folks to drop by again because they've forgotten something. Coffee?"

"Yes, please." I sit and let my gaze glide over the lake. From where I'm sitting on the deck, I can see all the way to the other side, even spotting the landing of my family's cabin.

"Here you go." She plants a steaming mug in front of me. "This shouldn't take long." My eyes follow her as she struts back inside with a light sway of her hips.

Friendship, I repeat over and over in my head. Friendship is good, anything more will distract me from the reason I came here.

Five minutes later Kay deposits a large plate of scrambled eggs in front of me, flanked by two slices of dark rye bread.

"Gosh," I murmur. "Are we sharing?"

"Nope." She sits opposite me, cradling a mug of coffee in her hands. "What have you been eating since you arrived?"

The eggs are delicious, creamy but not too runny, with just the right amount of seasoning, leaving a hint of something spicy on my tongue. "Oh my god," I exclaim, ignoring her question. "You're a domestic goddess."

"I know how to make eggs." Her tone is flat, but her eyes sparkle.

My hangover retreats as I wolf down the eggs. "I'm not much of a cook. No one in my family is, really. Although Mom seems to be into baking cakes lately."

"Will you come out with me tonight?"

The piece of bread I'm chewing gets stuck in my throat. I

cough to loosen it and swallow slowly to hide my shock. "What?"

"I don't mean *out-out*. It's just that, after the conversation we had last night, I feel it's my duty to take you on a tour of Northville's finer spots."

Both disappointment and relief surge inside me. I draw my lips into a pensive pout.

"I don't mean a bar crawl, Ella. Just a drive in my truck. A few stops along the way. I know just where to go to make you fall in love with this place all over again."

"How can I say no after you fed me eggs like that?" All the worry I carried for years seems to slip off me for that instant.

"That's what I figured." She cocks her head. "Nostalgia, here we come."

"Look, Kay, about the things I said last night…" She doesn't interrupt, just stares at me with an amused smile on her lips. "I didn't mean to be insensitive in any way. If anyone should understand, it's me. I, uh—" I had truly expected her to interrupt me at this point, what with her take-no-prisoners attitude, but she lets me talk freely—lets me get stuck in my own train of thought. "I didn't mean to imply anything or claim that one way of life is better than the other."

"Are you done?" She lets her eyes slide from my face to the empty plate in front of me. "I mean with your food. I know you'll never be done saying sorry, so you can just go on while I take these dishes into the kitchen." She stands and leans over the table. "No offense, Little Ella, but I'm truly not interested in your millions of excuses for everything."

Flabbergasted, I watch her saunter off again. Through the open door, I hear dishes clatter into the sink. For someone who grew up finding an explanation for every little action I undertook, Kay's approach is wildly refreshing.

"Shall we meet at six?" She reappears in the doorway. "No need to dress up."

———

Kay's driving style mirrors her personality: calm, confident, relaxed. She has one elbow propped out of the open car window, while her other hand rests on the steering wheel. We zip through the streets of Northville, mostly lined by houses just like the one I grew up in—the same place where my parents have lived for more than fifty years.

"Well, I surely wasn't expecting that." I give her a smirk when she pulls up alongside the woods skirting the edge of town.

"Just wait." From the backseat, Kay unearths a tote bag, the neck of a wine bottle peeking through its opening.

In this light—dying, the sun low—the woods have a dream-like quality, as if anything could happen. The air is cooler and damper between the trees. Kay leads the way to the clearing where I expect she'll stop. Only, she doesn't. She takes a left at the picnic bench where every inhabitant of Northville must have enjoyed an alfresco lunch at some point in their lives.

Next thing I know, I'm climbing a steep little hill. Once again I'm confronted with how out of shape I am, my breath wheezing in my lungs as we make our way up. Another left and then… The memory hits me hard and fast. Nancy Moore. Tenth Grade. She'd just gotten her driver's license and we used to drive to the woods after school and—

I watch Kay pull a blanket from the bag and spread it out over the ground.

"How did you know?" I ask, because this can't be a coincidence.

"Small town. You know how it goes." Kay gives a quick

nod with her head. "Why don't you sit down. The view is wonderful from here, as I'm sure you remember."

I had prepared myself for some gentle nostalgia, for a few bouts of joyful reminiscing about mutual acquaintances and how they had fared—Kay being a well of information— but I am not ready for this mind fuck. I feel tricked, fooled even. "B-but," I stammer.

"Do you really think you and Nancy were the only ones smart enough to figure out the beauty of this spot? Half the teenage population of Northville came here for the exact same reason you did." She starts fiddling with a corkscrew and the bottle. "If it makes you feel any better, my first time happened here too."

I sit on the blanket and overlook the valley below. Nancy Moore was the first girl who broke my heart.

"I see Nancy at The Attic sometimes. She remembers you fondly." Kay offers me a plastic cup of red wine. "It's from the winery in Fairfax. I'll take you there if you like it."

The wine may taste divine, but if it does, it doesn't get through to me. "You see Nancy?"

After digging a little hole in the ground to keep the bottle upright, Kay installs herself next to me, legs folded under her bottom, staring out into the distance. "I see everyone who hasn't left."

"How is she?" Nancy with the dimples in her cheeks I used to trace my finger along in this very spot.

"Married to Tommy Waterman. Three children. Works in the mayor's office, just like her daddy used to."

"God, that was such a long time ago." A small smile starts breaking through the stern, shocked expression on my face. "I haven't been here in, erm, twenty-two years."

"These days, kids don't come here anymore. So many more interesting things to do, you know? Facebook, video games, internet porn…"

"It's gorgeous." My muscles relax into the moment and the taste of the wine explodes in my mouth. "So impossibly green." The exact same thing I used to think when I came here with Nancy in the summer of 1990, listening to Roxette and Sinead O'Connor tapes on our Walkmans, unable to share one device because they only made one type of head-phones back then.

Already, I had wanted to leave. Because I knew it wouldn't last, knew I was just a temporary distraction for Nancy, who couldn't shut up about Drew Hester, even when it was just the two of us down here, her hand in my hair—and my heart in my throat.

She ignored me for weeks after I started dating him, but never breathed a word about the activities, though innocent enough, she and I had engaged in behind everyone's back.

"I was eighteen," Kay says. "Brett Dinkle was a real gentleman about it. Not a bad word to say about him. We stayed together for two more years after." She turns to me. "Are you a gold star, Little Ella?"

"No." As the sun dips lower behind the trees, the atmosphere changes to one of camaraderie, of forgotten hopes and dreams, and—apparently—intimate questions. "I tried. Because I felt I had to, I guess. I even had a proper boyfriend in college. It lasted a startling seven months, but, looking back—even as far back as the times I came here with Nancy—it should have been so crystal clear." In my heart, I always knew.

"It's not easy." Kay's voice is as serious as I've ever heard it. "Sophomore year, I had a massive crush on your sister."

Inadvertently, my eyebrows shoot up. "On Nina? Seriously?"

"She was the coolest girl in high school. I figured everyone had the hots for her, but, after discreetly inquiring, it turned out I was the only one of my female friends who felt that way." There's a hint of bitterness in her chuckle. "For some bizarre reason, for the most part of my teenage years, I considered it the most normal thing in the world. I just automatically assumed that attraction was fluid for everyone. Boy, was I wrong."

I want to say something deep and meaningful, but I'm still hung up on the crush she just confessed to having had on my sister.

As if reading my mind, Kay cocks her head and asks, "You really never hear from her?"

"Hardly. It breaks Mom and Dad's hearts, but really, they can't just sit around and pretend they had nothing to do with it."

"She was always a wild one, I'll tell you that. Definitely not made for sticking around in this town."

"Try being her sister." I knock back the last of the wine in my cup and hold it out for a refill. *An entire family's expectations pinned on you.* "And then having to tell your parents you're gay."

Kay pours more wine in silence, the dusk around us quickly turning into darkness. From the bag, which appears to be bottomless, she produces three stick candles, plants them in the ground and lights them from a match.

"I thought I was well-organized, but damn, you surprise me, Kay." I change the subject.

"You? Well-organized?" Kay shakes her head. "You're such a city girl, used to take-out dinners and everything being done for you. Give me a break." There's no malice in her voice and a bubble of laughter explodes from her throat after she says the words. "Who takes care of you back home?"

"No one." The emptiness of Boston seems so far away. "I mean, I have a cleaner, but that's it." Sonia, who found me.

"It's a different life, I guess." Kay balances her cup on the corner of the blanket and leans back on her hands. "No time to cook your own meals, to do your own dishes. What kind of life is that?"

"Who does dishes these days anyway?"

She fixes her eyes on me. "I do."

"Of course you do." The giggles that burst inside of me lift me up to heights I haven't reached in years.

"Remember truth or dare?" She draws her lips into a smirk.

"The movie or the game?"

"Wasn't the game inspired by the movie?" Kay pushes herself up and rubs the creases out of the skin of her hands. "Entertaining bored, hormonal teenagers across the country. And, if Nancy is to be believed, especially one Ella Goodman."

"I loved that movie. The money I would have given to see the Blonde Ambition tour live. To witness that moment Madonna drops her jacket in 'Express Yourself' with my own eyes. I believe my love for blazers may well stem from that."

"Thank goodness it stopped there and you didn't go for cone bras next."

A hysterical bout of laughter rumbles beneath my stomach, pulsing in my abs, and while the first howl escapes me, I punch Kay playfully in the biceps.

"Go on then. Truth or dare?"

"What?" As the convulsions in my gut subside, I stare at her in disbelief.

"Let's play. For nostalgia's sake."

I take another sip of wine and turn my entire body so I can face her better. "Truth."

Kay draws her features into a pensive pout. "When did your last serious relationship end?"

I huff out a breath of air. "No need to make such a spectacle to ask me that." Our gazes cross briefly. Her eyes flicker in the light of the candles, but she doesn't flinch. "Define serious."

"Don't give me that, Ella. Surely you're old and wise enough to distinguish a serious relationship from a fling or a one-night-stand. You're a professor, for heaven's sake."

"I don't have the best track record with relationships. I seem to have this tendency to drive women I like away. I'm not the easiest person to live with, what with having inherited my mother's flair for criticism and my dad's tendency to repress frustrations."

I shuffle around nervously on the blanket in the silence that follows after what I've just said.

"Are you always so hard on yourself?" Kay's soft tone pierces through the darkness that falls like lead around us.

The pure joy that raced through me earlier, that made me burst out in spontaneous laughter, has fled and left me with only tears stinging behind my eyes. I sniffle, and it sounds loud in the complete quiet surrounding us.

"I think I would like to go back now."

"Why?" Kay scoots closer and puts a hand on my knee. "Hey, come on." She locks her eyes on mine. "I thought you came back here for a reason?" Her fingers are light on my jeans. "How is more running away going to help?"

"You, uh, you don't understand. You don't know." I start pushing myself up, removing Kay's hand from my knee, knocking over my cup of wine and spilling the remainder of its contents in the process.

"All right. I'll take you back." In a flash, she stands up.

"I'm sorry," I begin to say, but remember how she told me off again this morning.

With methodical movements, ignoring the wine stain I left on it, Kay starts folding up the blanket, pushes the cork back in the bottle, blows out the candles, stuffs everything in the bag, and takes my hand. "Come on."

Through the dark, my hand in hers, we make our way back to the car. Regret courses through me—the familiar tightening in my chest, a lump the size of my heart pulsing in my throat.

6

That night, I dream of Nina playing a part in The Hobbit. She's one of the glamorous elves that were in the movie but not in the book. One who falls for the dwarf—always the wrong man.

When I wake at six I put on my bikini and head straight for the water. I swim from one end of the lake to the other and back, until I have to catch my breath, my elbows propped on the landing, my body doubled-over.

Thalia's voice swirls through my head. *You could have made more effort.* She'd introduced me to some of her work colleagues, people I had found absolutely nothing in common with—creative advertising types who spoke quickly and visited the wash room a bit too frequently—resulting in dire silence on my end. When I'd come for her after we got home, ignoring her remarks, she'd pushed me away. *You're not that good, Ella. This will not work.*

An approaching splash of water pulls me from my reverie. Kay's having her morning swim earlier than usual. With small strokes, she paddles toward me and pushes herself onto the landing in one swift movement. Water

47

cascades off her nut-brown skin, leaving it glistening in the early morning light.

"You're early." My skin is so pale next to hers. My arms so puny.

"What can I say, Ella? You've been on my mind." Her tone is easy as she stares down at me. "Don't worry, not in that way." A deep chuckle rumbles up from her chest. "You may as well walk around with a 'Do Not Touch' sign hanging from your neck. Or 'Emotionally Unavailable' or something like that."

Kay has bestowed so many small kindnesses on me since I arrived, I know it's my turn to give something back. "Her name was Thalia. We were together, albeit on and off, for about a year. It ended months ago."

Kay shakes some drops of water from her hair. They land on her shoulders and slowly drip down the curve of her upper arms.

"Was that really so hard?" The radiance of her smile momentarily floors me. *Before*, this would have been the moment I made my move.

I grin up at her, ignoring the memory of Thalia. After pushing myself out of the water, in not nearly as elegant a fashion as Kay, I sit next to her.

"It's all so complicated." Again, a swirl of thoughts in my brain. Not one of them can I articulate accurately.

"Why?" Our thighs meet in a slippery, wet touch. "Tell me about Thalia. What happened?" If it weren't for the sun's first rays reflecting off the water in front of me, its surface broken by the ripples Kay and I create with our toes, I would believe myself to be in Dr. Hakim's office.

"I met her at the opening of an exhibition of her paintings. Just a hobby. She's the creative director at Stiglitz & Stuart, but in her spare time she paints pictures. Very bright and colorful, almost child-like. Birds with big heads, that kind of stuff. I was really drawn to her work, bought a piece. We got talking. I fell in love." I can't suppress the sigh that escapes me. "It was good for—by my standards—quite a while. Six months of happiness, until the real me started rearing its head. My shrink says it's because I don't feel worthy of another woman's love, I call it self-sabotage."

"What's the difference between the two?" Kay's shoulder slams lightly into mine. I'm grateful she doesn't query me further on the mention of a shrink.

I shrug off her remark, echoes of Dr. Hakim's voice in my head. "I guess you could say I've been unsuccessfully dating women for about twenty years now. That's a lot of accumulated heartache."

"It's strange how, when I ask you a fairly straightforward question, you always end up going on a rant against yourself."

Not wanting a repeat performance of what happened last night, I playfully tap her ankle with mine. "Then let's stop talking about me. Tell me about you."

"Oh, Ella." Under water, our toes touch briefly. "You're doing my head in. But yes, please, let me school you in the art of conversation. Ask me a question and I'll give you a straight answer."

"When did *your* last serious relationship end?"

"Two years ago. He fell in love with someone else. These things happen. It hurt, no doubts there, and it was messy and painful, but I know it wasn't my fault. We still see each other sometimes."

"Did he cheat on you?" The question's out before I can even consider its inappropriateness.

"No. If he had, we probably wouldn't be on speaking terms again now. It was hard on him as well, but sometimes you meet someone you simply need to have. No life imaginable without them—no matter who you hurt in the process."

"God, you're so philosophical about that."

"I wasn't always. Time has passed. Wounds have healed. Life goes on." She turns to me and fixes her eyes on me. "Has that ever happened to you? That you met someone and you realize you'd regret it for the rest of your life if you didn't pursue them?"

"Many times."

Her gaze on me is intense.

"Really?" Her eyebrows shoot up. "I guess everyone is different."

"What? Why do you say that?"

"I'm not talking about mild infatuation here, Ella. I'm talking love that alters the course of your life. Love you would sacrifice everything for. Jeff sacrificed his life with me to be with that other woman, because he was certain he had no other choice—because it was his path in life. Despite the pain it caused me, I had to respect that."

"Jesus. How long were you and him together?"

"Six years." She flicks a wet strand of hair away from her forehead. "I hope you get the point I'm trying to make." A slight tilt of the head.

This must be how my students feel when I ask them a nearly impossible question at an exam.

"Sure." I'm not certain I like the preachy side of Kay that much.

"Fine, then." The serious expression on her face transforms into a smile, changing the mood of the moment from dark to light. "I'd better get back. What are you doing today?"

I haven't really given it much thought. "Don't know. Maybe stop by my parents."

"Good idea. I'll be here tonight if you want to talk." Kay lowers herself back into the water, shoots me a wink before she sets off, and swims away in the other direction.

All of this before 7 a.m. At least I'll have something to talk about with my parents. I need all the information they have on Kay Brody.

———

"Jeff Mitchum is a good guy," Dad says.

"Just because he buys you a beer now and then, doesn't make him a good man," Mom quickly jumps in.

"What would you know, Dee? Have you ever even had a decent conversation with him?"

"I don't need to have a conversation with him to see what kind of person he is, leaving his long-term partner for another woman, breaking up Linda's family in the process." Mom's tone is harsh—a notch up from her default one. No surprises there. I'm already regretting having asked about Kay. Instinctively, I go quiet and retreat from the conversation. Pretend I'm not there, the way I did when I was a child. Instead of listening, I study their faces. The thin lines of Mom's lips, the set of her chin—which resembles mine. Dad's bottomless blue eyes I inherited. And I know we share much more than a physical resemblance. All the things I hold against them, I may as well hold against myself.

What am I doing inquiring with my parents about Kay, anyway? She's never given me anything but an honest reply to every question I asked her. The last thing I should do, is use her as a topic of conversation with my parents. It's as much an escape as anything I do, a distraction from what really matters.

"I've been spending quite some time with her." This stops their pointless, never-ending row. I'm sure they'll pick it back up once I leave, but at least, for now, they've been silenced.

"You do know she's, uh—" Try as she might, my mother can't get the word across her lips.

"Bisexual?" I pull up my shoulders. "Of course I do."

"Running around with all sorts after Jeff left her. Not very discreet about it either," Dad chimes in. "Very unbecoming for a woman."

"For a woman?" Instantly, my irritation level peaks.

"Well, it was a bit much, the way she was carrying on with that girl. All up in everyone's face like that," Mom adds.

I sit there stunned. Not only, because for once in their lives, they seem to agree on something—the only previous instance of this that springs to mind is when I came out and they both insisted that I couldn't be sure, that I shouldn't 'swear off' men just yet, surely it was just a phase—but mainly because of their ignorant, hypocritical, narrow-minded nature on full display. *Am I like this?* These people's blood runs in my veins, their ideas have been planted in my head from a young age.

"Just stop it. The pair of you." I can't bite back my anger.

Not used to an outburst from their 'good daughter', they both stiffen.

"Listen to yourselves, really. Who made you so qualified to judge others? To look down on them from your moral high ground?"

"Darling, come on. It was just talk." My mother's mouth is drawn into a defeated pout.

"You weren't here to see, Ellie. She'd come to The Attic and sit canoodling with this girl from out of town," Dad says.

Red mist in front of my eyes. Rage like a cold fist in my chest. All the reasons why I left compressed in one moment.

With a brusque movement, I shove my chair back and walk out. My hands tremble on the steering wheel as I start the car, and all the while, all I can think of is Kay's bravery.

7

B ack at West Waters, only marginally calmed down, I slip out of my clothes, into my bikini and dive into the water. Its coolness strips me of at least one layer of anger, but I need to swim at least half a lap before my head clears and I can appreciate my surroundings. I let the bright green beauty of Oregon in late summer back into my heart, let it erase the agitation inside of me. Because this is not a new experience by a long stretch. It's an endlessly repeated cycle. The profound misunderstanding and miscommunication between me and my parents.

When I was thirteen and still firmly in my mother's camp, I once asked her why she stayed with my dad if he made her so unhappy. My friend Kelly's mom had gotten a divorce, much to Kelly's relief.

"What makes you think I'm unhappy, Darling?" she asked, a wry smile on her face.

I was so taken aback by this question, that I let the subject drop there and then—and adjusted my idea of happiness on the spot.

When I stop to take a breather at Kay's side of the lake, I

see her perched on a chair outside the lodge. She puts the book she is reading to the side and instantly walks over.

"And?" She crouches down and runs her fingers through the water. "Do I need to make you dinner tonight?" A tank top hangs loosely from her frame and—my breath stalls momentarily when I notice—she's not wearing a bra. I force myself to look her straight in the face.

"A few beers will do."

"Not when you come to my house." Her smile is bright, a glitter of something else—something I can't read—in her eyes.

"More truth or dare?" I blink up at her.

Her belly laugh has already become a source of comfort. "You just wait until I dare you." Kay stretches her legs and glares down at me. "Come by whenever you want. I'm home."

Swimming back, I can't get the image out of my head: as she pushed herself up, Kay's tank top twisted to the side an inch, offering me a delicious peek at the curve that lay beneath.

———

When I knock on the open door of Kay's place a few hours later, her bra-less outfit has been replaced by another v-neck t-shirt, so light the lines of her bra come through. I'm more relieved than disappointed—I know a distraction when I see it. Not that her welcoming, carefree smile doesn't knock me sideways a little bit.

"There's no one else here today. Not even Uncle Pete. He's on his annual pilgrimage to Portland to see his nephews. It's always like this after Labor Day. People suddenly become too busy, as if their switch has been flipped from relaxed to frantic."

We sit on the deck, a sliver of moon already overhead, the remnants of a scrumptious seafood salad in a bowl on the table, the bottle of Pinot I brought sitting almost empty between us.

"But honestly, for me—" Kay seems to be in a contemplative mood, lots of chatter, no probing questions just yet. "—who has lived here forever, the first half of September is the most gorgeous. Just before the leaves start turning. One last burst of summer. As if the trees are trying extra hard to give us one last hurrah. Look at that one over there." She points at a lush Chinkapin with long high branches stretching over the lake. "I bet you don't see trees like that in Boston."

The mention of my city—the place where it happened— pulls me out of the moment. The Chinkapin is old and statuesque and regal, but I can't see it the way Kay does. I can acknowledge its beauty and the sense of gravitas, the unspeakable splendor of nature, it lends to this particular corner of West Waters, but my train of thought has taken flight to my town house in Back Bay, with its small but green —and ecologically sustainable—back yard, which I'm now contemplating selling.

"No." I refill our glasses. "It's marvelous."

"Don't sound so convinced." A crooked smirk has slipped onto Kay's face.

"Hey—" I look around me, at the last of the sun bathing the lake in its orange evening glow, and the leaves lazily swaying in the breeze. "—I love it here. I truly do." I love it for its disconnectedness from everything, for its profound stillness at night, and its pureness in the first light of dawn.

"I take it you'll be staying a while."

"I'm only expected back at work after Christmas break." The months of nothingness spreading out in front of me fill me with a warm glow of dreamy joy—only a smidgen of fear piercing through my wine buzz.

"I'm honored you chose West Waters." She sips again, only briefly letting her eyes rest on me. "And I enjoy your company."

I was only just coming down from not being able to count my remaining days off on all twenty of my fingers and toes, when Kay's impromptu comment lifts me straight up onto another cloud. "Not infringing too much on your preference for solitude?"

"Contrary to what you may think, I'm not a solitary person. I live here, a few miles out of town, because it's my home and I'd be foolish not to—and I have absolutely no qualms about being alone—but I enjoy other people's company a great deal." A solemn note has crept into her voice. "I wouldn't have decided to take over the management of West Waters if I didn't."

"Fair enough." I let my gaze drift over the lake. "I was possibly just projecting. I'm not that good with people myself. Nine times out of ten, I always manage to say the wrong thing."

"But you're a teacher?" I feel Kay's stare, but don't look at her. "You must possess some social skills."

"I think I have the basics down." I turn to her, a grin on my face—the power of deflection. "And I have excellent TA's."

She slants her head, her gaze lost in the small distance between us for an instant. "Are you out at work?"

"More or less, I guess."

"What does that mean?" Kay draws up her eyebrows in an expression of puzzled bewilderment.

"I've never explicitly told anyone, but I presume it's understood."

"You presume? How does that work?" She taps her

fingers on the table. "I honestly don't understand. Please explain, Professor."

"I never bring a date to official college functions or colleagues' dinner parties. I don't bring up my personal life much. I don't wear frivolous lady dresses that often. This is the year 2014. People can put two and two together. Why would I spell it out for them?"

Kay's eyebrows do a funny dance: from all the way up, to knitted into a frown just above her eyes. She doesn't immediately speak, just sits there contemplating in silence. "I guess, ultimately, it depends on your motive. If you choose not to come out because it's nobody's business, that's fair. But if you don't do it because you're ashamed, what kind of example is that to your students?"

"Ashamed?" To my horror, my father's words from earlier that day run through my head. Would I ever bring a woman to The Attic—or any bar in Boston where I had any chance of running into fellow faculty members, or students —and openly 'canoodle' with her?" Admittedly, I have too much shame and guilt in my life, but not because I'm a lesbian." I shake my head to emphasize my point. "Never for that."

"What if, with being openly gay at Boston U, you could change someone's life just by being yourself and showing them it's okay? Don't we owe that to every non-heterosexual person that came before us and fought much worse wars than we ever had to?"

"I hadn't pegged you for an activist." Nervously, I tap my foot to the wood of the deck. "But, first of all, I'm not there to change my students' lives or to make them feel better about themselves. I'm there to teach them a subject. My personal life is private."

"And?" Kay's lips are pursed together in a tight pout.
"And what?"

"You said 'first of all', I can't wait to hear your second point."

"I don't mean to be insensitive, but you're bisexual. It's different for you. From what I hear, you only turn to girls to nurse a broken heart, anyway."

"From what you hear?" Kay's eyes have narrowed to slits.

In the moment of stunned silence that hangs between us, I realize I'm behaving just like the people who raised me. Quick to judge and ignorant. My head up my own ass. Expressing the joylessness of my existence through frustrated statements like the one I just made.

"I'm sorry." The regret that courses through me has a paralyzing effect on my brain. More emotions than I can adequately express ganging up on me. "I shouldn't have said that. I didn't mean it." Then the tears, always my first response to my own feelings of powerlessness. "God." I shake my head. "I don't expect you to accept my apologies. If I were in your shoes, I wouldn't either—"

"Ella. Stop." Kay bounces the fingers of one hand against the palm of the other. "Time out."

"I'm so stupid sometimes." I start to get up.

"This is not an all or nothing situation. You said something in the heat of the moment. You made a mistake, you didn't instigate the end of the world. No one died." She nods at my chair with a swift flick of the head. "Sit down, please."

Because I have no earthly idea what else to do, I crash back down in my seat, my body glad for the support the chair offers.

"I'm sorry. I'm such a mess." I mumble it more to myself than I'm saying it to her.

"Truth be told, I've come to expect a certain degree of ignorance from some folks in Northville, but yours has taken me by surprise somewhat."

"It's not—I'm not like that, Kay." I tap my chest. "In

here. I'm not. I just—" But it's too difficult to put into words. The conflict between who and what I am and the relentless desire, despite everything that stands between us, to please my parents. To make up for what I've done. To have them speak of me with pride in their voices again. And how I utterly, completely failed them—not because I'm a lesbian, but because of the message of total weakness I sent. The phone call they received that must have made their world cave in. How I despise myself for it.

When I look up at Kay this time, stealing a furtive glance, I don't see the acceptance and warmth I've come to know from her. And I understand, because I'm just a stammering, broken shadow of a woman. Someone who has come to hide on her premises. Just like everyone else in this world, she doesn't owe me anything.

"What happened to you, Ella?"

"No." On automatic pilot, I shake my head. "I can't."

"When has 'No, I can't' ever helped you?"

It rings truer than I want it to. "Never." As night comes, more silence surrounds us.

"Okay, if you don't want to talk, that's fine. Why don't I do the talking?" She stretches her arm out over the table top. "Just don't run away again. Stay. Sit here for a while." Her fingertips have reached my hand. "With me." She doesn't touch me, she's just there and I wish I knew how to express my gratitude, but the dryness in my throat is an accurate reflection of the turmoil in my brain. The thoughts that keep on going, the blame that never shifts.

"Okay." I nod, and cover her hand in mine.

8

Heat glows in my veins as, over another bottle of Pinot, I listen to Kay's story of how her father wooed her mother. I remember Mr. Brody from when I came to West Waters as a child, how his eyes always glinted when he spoke of his wife. Unflinching pride and endless respect. Not something very common in my own family's house, not now and not then.

"After Mom died, he just faded away." Kay's voice breaks a little. "I don't believe in it medically, but I truly think he died of a broken heart. I witnessed it with my own eyes. Saw the straightness seep from his gait, the light leave his eyes. He didn't speak with the same voice after she was gone. And as much as it hurt me to see him like that, I knew it wasn't weakness. It was love. He simply couldn't live without her."

She fixes her moist eyes on me. "Can you imagine that, Ella? To love another human being with so much intensity it literally kills you when they die?"

I shake my head because I have absolutely no idea what that must be like. I can't help but wonder what Dr. Hakim would have to say about that.

"The last thing he said to me was: 'Find someone you love.' It was all he ever wanted for me, to find love the way he had. He didn't care about degrees and any of that; he just wanted me to be happy above all else. When I was little and he'd put me to bed, he'd always ask me if I'd had a good day. If what I had done had made me happy. Not if I had achieved something extraordinary, or done well on a test, or made him proud by winning something insignificant. Only happiness mattered. That feeling here"—she taps her chest —"of a content soul."

"What a wonderful thing to teach a child." I squeeze the words out of my throat, wholly overwhelmed by the emotion in Kay's voice. I wish I could contribute a story of my own, of the values my parents taught by setting an example, but I draw a blank.

To accept yourself fully, Ella, Dr. Hakim would say, *to get through this, you must learn to respect where you came from.* But, compared to Kay's stories of love and happiness, the house I spent the first seventeen years of my life in might as well have been a cold war zone.

"He loved West Waters. It made him happy and, in the end, it's a comforting thought. Neither one of my parents grew to be old, but at least they were fiercely happy for most of their lives. They had each other, this place, and me. Even my mother, who was quite different, much more pragmatic and realistic—not that much of a romantic dreamer—used to tell me that." She raises her glass. "To Mabel and Patrick Brody."

With an unsteady hand, I clink my glass to hers. "You must miss them a lot."

"I do." With a quick flick of her thumb, Kay prevents a tear from dropping out of the corner of her eye. "But, I guess, what stings the most is that I obviously haven't found the love that Dad used to refer to. The kind that lasts a lifetime." She huffs out a breathy chuckle. "Sometimes, I wonder if he was completely sane, you know? If he experienced emotions that weren't humanly possible. But still, it's a good dream to have, something to aspire to." She clears her throat. "Which is also why, in the end, I couldn't hold a grudge against Jeff for leaving me. He found that kind of love, or something close to it. And the fact that him leaving me didn't kill me, is proof that, perhaps, he wasn't the one I would love forever, anyway." Out of nowhere, she cracks a smile. "It's good to be philosophical about certain things. Better than letting them destroy you."

Of all the things I expected to find here—helpful nostalgia, a connection to a happy time in my life, peace and quiet for my ever-churning brain—life lessons from Kay Brody were the last thing on my list. And I do feel a connection, not to the time when I was a child, but to the here and now, to her.

"There's only one activity that can appropriately end a night like this." Kay swallows the last of her wine and firmly deposits her glass on the table.

Expectantly, I arch up my eyebrows.

"Enough babbling, Ella. We need to get naked." She flashes me a wide smile, her white teeth glinting in the feeble night lights on the lodge's deck.

"We need to what?" Fear and a tingle of something alien, but exciting, mingle in my blood.

Kay points at the lake. "Time for skinny-dipping." She fixes her gaze on me. "This is no time to be a prude either, Little Ella. But, seeing as you probably will be, I'll go first and I won't look when you jump in." There's that wink again.

I watch Kay as she heads toward the water's edge, already pulling her t-shirt over her head. Carelessly, she tosses it to the ground. Her bra soon follows, as do her shorts and underwear. The lake is only a few yards from the deck, but unlit at this time of the evening, and from where I'm sitting—still flabbergasted—Kay's naked body is just a silhouette getting ready to dive in. She does so with an elegant splash, barely ruffling the water's surface and, as promised, she doesn't turn around.

How did we go from talking about deceased parents to night swimming? As usual, my brain is coming up with a million reasons a minute to not strip and jump in after Kay—second nature, really. But I feel the pull of the water, I sense its allure. It's stronger than the doubts quickly accumulating in my brain—and the wine helps.

Almost like an out-of-body experience, I hoist my top over my head, leave my shorts on the deck and, barefoot, saunter toward the lake. I stand there for a few seconds, only clad in my underwear. Kay's swimming toward the middle of the lake, giving me the privacy I need. I scan my surroundings. Is there really no one around?

But the only sound is the water splashing around Kay in the distance, a light rustle in the leaves because of the evening breeze, and my breath, which comes quickly and ragged.

I fold my arms around my back and unhook my bra, yanking down my panties when I let it slip off my body, leaving my underwear in a puddle of cotton fabric by the lake. I stand naked in front of the water, ready to jump in and swim after Kay. And I feel a warm fuzz of contentment wrap itself around my heart.

Freed, I dive in. The water glides along my body, cleansing me in an exhilarating, midnight-swim way. There's nothing like moving through water completely naked, without the confines of tight swim gear. No barriers. Just nature surrounding me. In the deafening silence of the night, I make my way toward Kay. She has reached the western edge of the lake, where we watched the sun dip behind the trees earlier, treading water.

"There's nothing like it, is there?" She's just a shadow in the darkness, but her voice, already so familiar, soothes me.

"It's amazing." I let my head fall back, my ears underwater, my nipples momentarily peeking out over the surface, but I don't care. The breeze rushes over them and I feel it shoot through my entire body. For the first time in a long while, I feel alive—and incredibly aroused. Tears stream down my cheeks when I tilt my body upward again. But it's dark and we're in the lake, surrounded by water anyway. I can see my cabin from here. The place I came to heal. And I know I have a lot of work to do, but right now, it doesn't matter. Right now, I just feel. The possibilities of life. A glimmer of happiness. What I would have missed.

I dive under briefly, erasing my tears, before swimming to the other end and back. When I let myself drift on my back, the stars above me, the water underneath, and Kay close by, I know I'm ready to talk.

9

Kay has brought out the whiskey and we sit, wrapped in soft bathrobes, on her deck again. I take a sip, and another.

"Good stuff, huh?" She eyes me quizzically. "There's something different about you. You seem more at ease after that swim." A smile slides along her lips. "Are you catholic? Was it like being baptized all over again?"

Silently, I shake my head and wait until she relaxes back into her seat, twirling her glass between her fingers. "What you asked me earlier. About what happened to me?"

"Yes." Kay nods.

"I gave up. On life. On everything." The soft, steady voice with which I proclaim the words surprises me. "Mainly on myself, because I was so sick of making the same mistakes over and over again, of repeating the endless cycle of a short peak of happiness—usually brought on by a delusional love affair, but not always—followed by an ever-growing darkness. So sick of putting on that mask every single day, of putting on that front. Of pretending that life was peachy." I pause to take another sip. The heat of the booze burns inside of me, marking the moment. It also allows me to continue to speak these words I've only—stutteringly, engulfed by bottomless shame and guilt—ever uttered in Dr. Hakim's office.

"To keep up that front takes everything you've got. After all, I was made professor long before my time was due. I had a house in Back Bay. The respect of my peers. Never short of attention from attractive women. I had every reason to be happy. When I looked at my life objectively, like an outsider, I could almost see it. But I never, ever felt it. Not longer than five minutes anyway—which was, quite possibly, the cruelest aspect of it. These fleeting glimpses of how it could be. Of how other people must go through life. Able to face adversity because of normal levels of self-esteem. Always ready to battle the downs because of this unstoppable zest for life. While I, with my PhD and promising career, wallowed in misery."

Kay leans forward in her chair, placing her elbows on the table, her hands close to mine.

"I didn't understand, so I studied it. Because that's what I do. I read dozens of books, some of which delivered the aha-moment I was so desperately looking for, lifting me out of my depression for short bursts of enlightenment, but all the knowledge in the world can't change your brain chemistry." I pause to let my gaze wander over the water, the effect it had on me, predictably, already wearing off.

"Unfortunately, I possess a very dramatic, hopeless streak. One that doesn't allow me to shrug things off and move on. I'm not resilient." A familiar pressure in my chest. "I'm weak." I try to take a deep breath. "And I went to great lengths to prove it." The way I burst into tears is how my forehead can burst out into a sudden sweat when running, instantly drenching, all of it raining down my skin at once. "Oh fuck." Pushing my palms against my eyes doesn't help.

"Hey, hey." In a flash, Kay is by my side. One hand

inside the robe, on my knee, the other stroking my arm. "You're not weak. You're brave."

I shake my head. "You don't know the half of it." It comes out as a howl, a cry for help too late to make a difference.

"You're here. That's what matters." Kay's voice is raw. Low. It sounds sort of undone. Her fingers knead the flesh of my knee.

"I'm sorry." I straighten my posture a little. "This… shouldn't be happening. You never asked for this."

"I did, though. I asked you what happened." With the sleeve of her robe, she catches a few tears on my cheek. But my emotional confession has left me numbed, and the significance of the moment passes me by. "Why don't we go inside? You can take a shower. You should stay in my guest room tonight."

"I haven't told you everything yet." For the first time since cracking, I look into her eyes.

"But you've told me more than enough." Endless kindness brims in her eyes.

"I need to tell you now. If I don't, I may never do it."

"Okay. Of course." Kay pushes herself up, leaving one hand on my shoulder while she speaks. "Let me just do some rearranging." As if it's made of the lightest plastic, she shoves the wooden table to the back of the deck, grabs her chair and sets it down where the table was, next to mine. She refills both our glasses, hands me mine, and sits, her face so close I can hear her breathe.

She doesn't ask me if I'm comfortable with her being so near—touching distance—just assumes she's doing the right thing. I like that about Kay. And I don't mind that her hand is hovering close to my exposed knee again, the coffee color of her skin contrasting starkly with the white fabric of the robe, even in the dark.

When I start speaking, my voice is small, because it's the only way it can be to say this. "When I said earlier that I gave up, I—" A sharp intake of breath, because admitting defeat out loud is never easy. Putting the moment I decided to let go into words—the moment I had never planned on recounting to anyone. "I meant that I tried to kill myself." I stare into my glass, into the dark-golden liquid. "Pills. My housekeeper found me. Maybe because I wanted her to. But, mainly, I just wanted to slip away. Leave unnoticed." I take a sip to relax my throat.

"When I woke up in the hospital, my friend Trish next to me in tears, all I felt was shame. I was so ashamed, in fact, that I pretended it was all a mistake. That I was fine. You know, employing tactics I learned from a very young age. For a while, I even made myself believe it. Checked myself out of the psych ward after three days with a big smile on my face. I couldn't feel anything except massive, obliterating shame. It eclipsed everything. Everyone knew better, except me."

Kay's hand is on my thigh, on top of the robe. She presses down hard with her fingers, possibly indicating that she understands. But someone who hasn't been there can never fully understand. The darkness. A despair so great there's no way out. And all the world sees is a coward who couldn't take it anymore. Just another someone who has taken the easy way out.

"I hadn't even really planned it. I'm a doctor of biology, I mean, I should know what can do the trick, right? But I could never bring myself to consciously think too much about it. It happened more in a haze. My brain encased in fluff, my body going through motions."

My thoughts start to scatter again. My mind jumping from one dazed memory to the next.

"Trish called my parents, of course. Which was not too

bad, because in my family we only believe firmly in one thing: ignorance is bliss." My usual chuckle at what should be emblazoned above my parents' front door doesn't happen. "Obviously, I couldn't keep up the charade. Returning to my house, to where it happened. Everything a blurry reminder, but a reminder nonetheless. My friends didn't let me get away with it either, so I ended up seeing Dr. Hakim, one of the best psychiatrists in Boston. He made me come up— because that's what they do, you see—with the idea to return home. And face the music, so to speak. Haven't heard a lot of music yet."

By the end of my speech, I feel detached from the words. A calmness runs through me. My breath has returned to normal and my chest feels loose and non-constricted.

"I said you were brave. Coming back here takes courage." Kay fixes her gaze on me, as if words are not enough. As though I need to see it in her eyes as well.

"I've been hiding out here, mostly. Enjoying this beautiful, idyllic place. Trying to forget, once again."

"You came, that's what's important. Take it one step at a time. You've just been acclimatizing, that's all."

I meet Kay's eyes. "You're not shocked or, at least, deeply appalled by my story?"

"No." There's a lot of power in the way Kay shakes her head. "Of course not." She removes her hand from my thigh and holds it open, palm up, inviting me to put my hand in hers. "Seems to me that, out of everyone, you're the one who's giving yourself the least credit." I touch her fingers with mine. "This one thing you did doesn't define you, Ella. It doesn't have to set the tone for the rest of your life."

With both of our defenses down, I see all of Kay's beauty on full display. "God, you're so together. So wise."

"And I didn't even go to college." Kay curls her fingers around mine, a small but confident smile on her lips. "Hey, I know you have a lot to deal with, but I'm here if you need me. Every step of the way."

Despite being touched by her kindness, I have to ask. "Why? You barely know me. You certainly don't owe me anything. I mean—"

"Does there have to be a reason for everything?" Kay doesn't let me finish. "I'm your friend now, Ella. It's what friends do."

"Just so you know—" I start choking up again. "I'm a bloody lousy friend."

"Why don't you let me be the judge of that." Eyes on me, Kay leans forward and plants a kiss on my forehead.

10

The next morning at breakfast—more of Kay's deliciously creamy scrambled eggs—I'm wrapped in silence. The whiskey knocked me out in the end, pushing me into a fitful sleep, but I'm still tired. Last night's conversation has drained all energy from my body.

Kay doesn't force small talk, as though she has a sixth sense about these things. She's all showered and dressed already, wearing jeans and a pale yellow blouse, I'm still in the robe she loaned me last night.

When my curiosity gets the best of me, I ask, "What's with the fancy-dress?" I've been here almost a week and I've never seen her in anything but shorts or slacks.

"Got some business to attend to today. Some potential tenants are viewing one of my properties."

One of her properties? The surprise must be visible on my face, because Kay breaks out into a smile and gives a chuckle. "My father didn't go to college either, but he knew that real estate is always the best investment." She shrugs. "I don't have expensive tastes, but West Waters barely makes me enough to get my hair cut every three months. And buy a new pair of denim shorts now and then."

"How many 'properties' have you got?" My interest is piqued.

"Just a few apartments in the building they constructed on the high street in the nineties. And The Attic."

"You own The Attic?" I have to keep my jaw from dropping all the way down to the table's surface.

"Bought it after Jeff left me. Bit of a bitter revenge situation at the time, but it has paid off well in the end."

It hits me that, last night, I poured the inner workings of my soul out to a woman I know hardly anything about.

"Jesus christ." I drop my fork onto my empty plate. "A woman of many talents."

"We all have bills to pay." Kay starts pushing her chair back. "And I'm mostly reaping the rewards of the smart decisions my father made." Towering over the table, she locks her gaze on mine. "I have some errands to run first. Feel free to use the bath, or anything else you may need. Just make sure the door's locked when you leave." She looks at me in silence for a few moments before inching closer and putting a hand in my neck. "See you later." A quick squeeze of her fingers, and she's gone.

Instantly, Kay's house feels too empty, allowing too much room for destructive thoughts. I want to stay longer, have a bit of a browse around, check out which books she reads and what she keeps in her refrigerator, but I can't. I have to get out of there now that she has left. It doesn't feel right anymore.

I locate my clothes in the living room, draped over the back of a chair. When I pick up my underwear, I can't help but think that Kay touched it when she put it there. *I'm your friend now,* she said. And perhaps she is, but I distinctly remember the shiver of arousal that came over me in the water, and I realize it wasn't just the freedom of skinny-dipping that caused it.

———

Verbalizing is a powerful, positive thing. Dr. Hakim's voice in my head again. But any relief I felt after telling Kay is slowly but surely being crushed by shame again. At least, in Dr. Hakim's office, I could leave the shame behind, if only for a few hours a week. I'm starting to miss his liver-spotted hands, his long fingers stroking that pitiful excuse for a goatee whenever I said something remotely meaningful. Out here, it's just me. And Kay. But that's different. And I know what he would say: *Steer clear of distractions, Ella. This is a pattern we're trying to break.*

When I arrive back at my own cabin, I take a long, hot shower before booting up my laptop and opening a draft e-mail to my sister. She's my flesh and blood—the only sibling I have—and she doesn't even know. At least *I* haven't told her. I can't be sure about my mother—whom I wouldn't put it past to use it to lure a response out of Nina. *Distorted negative thinking. Stop it.* Instead of letting my thoughts meander into that direction, I turn to the e-mail, which has been sitting in my drafts folder for weeks, and start typing. I compose an abridged version of what I told Kay, leaving out any criticism of our parents, and, before giving myself the chance to doubt—clearly remembering Kay's hand on my thigh and her warm, supportive response—hit send.

Of course, Nina is not Kay. I think of Kay's confession in the woods, about her teenage crush on my sister. I don't allow myself to acknowledge the pang of jealousy that shivers up my spine.

My phone, which I left on my night stand before leaving for Kay's the night before, only now pops up in my field of vision. Dr. Hakim would be proud of me for not being glued to it permanently. I have one missed call and a text message from my mother.

I would really like to come and see you at the cabin some time. Whenever suits you. Love, Mom.

It's only a short message but by the time I'm done reading it, the screen of my phone is a blurry mess behind my tears. And I know that as long as I can't read a text message from my mother without crying, I have a very long way to go.

Physically, I feel only the tiniest bit hungover, but emotionally, I feel very tender. Exposed. My secret is out. I'm not sure I can face my mother today, but a text message like that is as clear an invitation as I will ever get.

My mother, who used to be my hero—and whose fall from grace I witnessed with an incurable ache in my soul. I practiced the conversation I should have with her countless times in my head, and with Dr. Hakim, whose limitless patience, I suspect, is what makes him one of the best in his field. Most nights, I fall asleep reciting the words I should say. I know myself well enough to realize they'll never leave my lips the way I intend them to. That connection—from brain to tongue—has never worked very well for me.

It's always easier to not do something difficult. I have a note on my phone containing many of Dr. Hakim's parting words. I guess this one applies. I'll need to talk to my mother sooner or later—after having put it off for about twenty years. It's why I came here in the first place. I text her back, saying I will be at the cabin all afternoon. Immediately after I've sent it, a knot forms deep in my stomach.

My mother and I never talk. On the few occasions that I

made it back to Northville since leaving for college, I always went out of my way to make sure I never found myself alone in a room with her. I call her maybe once a month, the conversation dead after a few minutes, because, from behind the walls we have both put up, we have nothing to say to each other.

———

As soon as I lay eyes on her, it strikes me again that, at least physically, she's not the same woman anymore. Emaciated frame. Eyes as dull as the blackness I know so well. Face puffed up in all the wrong places because of too many pills she shouldn't be taking.

We don't hug, the courtesy embrace reserved for my return used up days ago. After she has sat down in one of the porch chairs, all I see is a woman gone wrong. A life wasted on all the wrong emotions. Hate. Bitterness. A twisted sense of duty.

I did it all for you and your sister. Not that I expect any gratitude in return, she once said. The familiar hint of blame in her voice, a hard edge in her tone that clings to it like a stain that can never be washed out.

As I pour us both a cup of coffee, I know that pity should not be the primary emotion bubbling to the surface when laying eyes on my own mother, but it's what I feel anyway. At least it's better than anger—the reigning sentiment in the Goodman house for as long as I can remember.

We both sit there, not knowing where to start. Even small talk seems too much, and neither one of us is very good at it.

"I've, uh, been seeing a psychiatrist for a few months now," I begin to say. "We both agreed it would be a good idea for me to come here."

"Oh, Ella, just tell me one thing." I know what she's

going to ask before the words leave her mouth. "Was it my fault?" The courage it must have taken her to formulate that question doesn't weigh up to the instant flash of anger that rises through me. Because I didn't come here to absolve anyone of guilt.

"No, Mom." My tone is sharp. "We all make our own choices and no one else is responsible for them except ourselves."

"I don't sleep anymore. Not even with a double dose of Ambien. I lie awake at night, twisting and turning. Thank goodness your father and I have been sleeping in separate bedrooms for years—although I can still hear him snore through the wall, especially on Thursdays and Fridays, after he's been to The Attic…"

A brand new silence descends on us after her short ramble. I want to say I'm sorry—because I'm infinitely sorry for what I did—but not like this. Not after she's just slipped on her coat of endless suffering and victimhood again.

"Oh hello, Mrs. Goodman." Kay steps into my field of vision, back in shorts and a t-shirt, and I could not be happier to hear her voice. Because, as much as I need to have a conversation with my mother, I don't want to have it now. Kay's sudden appearance is like a lifeguard's just as I'm about to drown. "How are you?"

"Kay," is all Mom says, and I can almost see the cogs in her brain turning. *Are they doing it? This bisexual woman and my daughter?*

"Care to join us?" I'm quick to ask, although it's hardly fair on Kay to invite her into our awkward non-chat. A glance passes between us, and in that instant, I know Kay will save me.

"Sure, if I'm not interrupting." She climbs the two stairs. "Good to see you, Mrs. Goodman. It's been a while."

Mom scoots her chair back a bit, so Kay can drag a third one closer and huddle around the table with us.

"Let me get you a mug. Or would you like something stronger?" I shoot up out of my chair.

"Coffee's fine," Kay says, easing into her seat, her face relaxed.

Despite Kay's calming presence, I need to take a deep breath while I grab the extra mug. Even a few minutes away from the stifling atmosphere that always hangs between my mother and me feels like a huge relief.

When I return, I see the relief on my mother's face because of Kay showing up as well. We share DNA, are cut from the same cloth, and she's probably just as grateful that our conversation was interrupted. And she got the answer she came here to get, anyway.

Mom and Kay chit-chat about the weather, the beauty of West Waters, and Uncle Pete, while I observe them silently. Every time my mother speaks, I hear my own voice—and, to my own dismay, it makes me cringe a little. Because, as much as I don't want to be like her, like a woman I've grown to pity more than respect, I am her daughter, and nothing has ever been more set in stone than that.

11

"I've seen her change too," Kay says, a few hours after Mom has left and we've moved our conversation to the lodge. "Over the years."

"Yeah, playing the victim doesn't really suit anyone." I bite down hard on the inside of my bottom lip, trying to fend off the wave of emotion that is coming loose again. "I used to really look up to her, while Nina was always more of a Daddy's girl. I guess, when it came out, she was at that delicate age where disappointment turns into destructive rage. One she, obviously, still hasn't recovered from."

I spot the look of puzzlement in Kay's eyes, but she doesn't probe.

"Dad had a mistress. A full-blown affair with someone from work. It lasted a year and, as Mom likes to remind us, if she hadn't found out, it might have gone on forever."

Kay's eyebrows shoot up. "John? Are you kidding me?"

"I know. You'd never have pegged him for the sort just by looking at him. A quiet, demure, hard-working man who never wished harm on anyone. Although it put the hours he spent at work into perspective, of course." I can grin at it now. I've spent years analyzing the possible motivations for my Dad to strike up a romance with another woman, always coming back to the same old reasons. I also know that, while it was the direct catalyst for the destruction of our family, at the core of it all, it wasn't the main reason.

"I was only thirteen and I didn't really understand what was going on, but Nina took it hard. He was her hero, you know? The guy she adored most in the world. After that, she went off the rails. Fell in with a bad crowd. Blew her college applications. It's hard to say why some people never bounce back. She's very much like Mom in that respect. Very proud. Extremely stubborn. Would rather hold on to a super-destructive grudge than forgive. Not budging an inch."

I glance at Kay. She has narrowed her eyes, appearing fully absorbed by the sordid details of my family's secrets.

"Mom made it seem as if she was making a huge sacrifice by not leaving him. By standing by his side and not kicking him out. That first year, not a day went by that she didn't rub it in all of our faces. Dee Goodman, the biggest person on the planet." I shake my head. "But let's just say that, from then on, dinner was quite a frosty affair. Every moment bathed in an accusatory silence and every word drenched in blame. They dealt with it the way they deal with everything: by not addressing it, by keeping up appearances at all costs, and by ignoring it until the problem goes away." I fix my eyes on Kay. "Have there never been any rumors about this in town?"

Kay shrugs. "It happened so long ago, but no, not that I know of." She spreads her arms. "And, growing up here, I've heard a lot of gossip. Even at an age when I wasn't supposed to." She flashes me a grin, her bright white teeth glittering in the dusk. "There was talk about Nina, of course. About her and the Hardy boy. How that turned out."

"The final nail in my Mom's coffin. God, you should

have heard her. As if all the suffering of the world had been piled upon her. 'After all I've done for this family.' Endless litanies like that. The problem with Mom is that she has always believed that she's the only one who ever had the courage to do the right thing. Not that it's all Mom's fault." I sigh deeply. "And now they're both retired, still living in the same house, spending most of their time together—well, minus the hours Dad spends at The Attic. Can you believe that?"

"True love and all that," Kay says in a sarcastic tone.

"Love?" I snicker. "If I know one thing in my life with absolute certainty, it's that love has nothing to do with it." I let my gaze drift over the water.

"Tough day today, Little Ella," Kay says, as if reading my mind again. "Swim?"

"God yes." I glower at Kay, unsure if she means a repeat of our nude night swimming session of the day before. Night hasn't fully fallen yet, and I'm a bit hesitant to shed all my clothes.

She pulls her t-shirt over her head, revealing the white bikini top that suits her skin tone so well.

"I'm not wearing my bathing suit." I watch Kay step out of her shorts and I feel it again. I feel glad to be alive.

"Just jump in in your underwear." Kay turns and leers at me. "Or naked." Coquettishly, she brings her hands to her hips. "You won't get any complaints from me." She walks to the water's edge and dives in.

Perhaps because of all the memories I've dug up today, and how everything about them seemed to be about being in control and curbing the sense of freedom needed for happiness, I take off all my clothes and, naked, jump in after Kay.

"Bold move, Goodman." Kay is treading water in the middle of the lake. "Not that I was watching."

With the water flowing all around me, unobstructed by

any fabric, I feel almost as one with the lake—and I never want to wear my bathing suit again.

As the sky turns a shade darker, I glare at Kay. She's so easy to be around. So uncomplicated. So pure. So everything I'm not.

"Thank you." The words bubble up from the bottom of my heart.

"For what?" Despite the darkness, I see the kindness in her eyes.

"Just for being you—and being here."

"Oh, Ella," she pauses for a split second, "you have no idea."

Before I have a chance to respond, she swims off in the other direction. Momentarily stunned, I watch her as the distance between us grows bigger, but I don't give her time to get away too far. I'm not as good a swimmer as Kay, and it takes a while before I catch up with her. I rest my elbows on the landing where she has chosen to rest, breathing in deeply to restore my heart rate to something acceptable.

"What did you mean by that?" I manage to puff out between sharp intakes of breath. Our elbows nearly touch.

"Nothing, really." Kay slowly turns her head to face me. "Nothing I could possibly burden you with right now, anyway." Something in her eyes has changed. As if, deep inside of her, a battle is raging, a fierce debate on whether to lower her defenses or not.

"Come on. I just shared the best kept Goodman family secret with you."

Under water, our feet bump into each other.

Her eyes still on me, our feet now a safe distance apart, she says, "I take it back. I shouldn't have said that."

"What? Why?" I feel the moment slipping away.

"Additionally, I could never tell you while your naked body is floating so close to me."

84

Suddenly, I'm very aware of my nipples and how hard they've become. How the water between my legs seems to pulse to the rhythm of my heartbeat.

"Never mind." Kay starts pushing herself out of the water, gulps of it cascading down her strong arms. "I'll get you a towel." I watch her totter off toward the lodge and I'm fairly certain of what she wanted to say. I feel it too, but, perhaps for different reasons, I can't say it either.

12

_____

The next day, I invite my father for a beer at The Attic. As close to home turf as it gets for him. It's the middle of the afternoon, and, apart from us, Joe the bartender, and a lone figure hunching over the bar, it's empty. At my request, Dad and I slide into a booth, waiting for our first beer before launching into anything resembling a conversation.

"Look, Ellie," he starts uncomfortably. "What I said the other day... heat of the moment stuff, you know?"

"It's fine, Dad." I dismiss his comment with a wave of my hand. Maybe it bothers him that Kay owns this place—possibly his favorite place in Northville. And that of the money he spends here treating his buddies, a considerable amount goes straight into her pocket. I try to empty my brain of assumptions. In my family, we hardly ever speak before thinking—often ending up not speaking at all because we think we have it all so figured out in our heads already, anyway.

"I've known Kay Brody since she was born. I know she's all right." Already, his eyes are watery—all the emotions he fails to express in words always surfacing there. "She hasn't had the easiest time, with both her parents passing so quickly after each other. And then the whole history with Jeff. It must have taken a toll."

"Kay is the most level-headed, honest, down-to-earth person I've met in a very long time." I choke up a bit as I say it.

Dad looks up, the question burning on the tip of his tongue. But Joe brings our beers, slapping both me and my father on the shoulder in some sort of awkward, friendly gesture. Dad takes a big gulp, his frame visibly relaxing.

"Is something going on between the two of you? I'm not asking so I can judge or give my opinion. I'm only asking because you're my daughter, Ellie. I feel as if I know nothing about you anymore."

My dad's forwardness takes me aback—and makes me wonder if he had a few shots of whiskey before coming here.

"No. We're friends." I try to keep my tone steady. "I didn't come here to fall in love." *But what if you do?* A voice in my head asks.

"I wouldn't expect you to tell your old dad even if something was blossoming between the two of you." Dad sends me a sad smile.

It's different talking to him. Although he carries a lot of anger inside of him as well, it's often obliterated by guilt—something I can relate to much easier than my mother's eternal victimhood.

As much as I would like to sit here all afternoon and discuss the merits of Kay Brody, I have a much more pressing matter to talk through with my dad.

"I'm worried about Mom." *Because I recognize the signs*, I want to add. "She came to see me yesterday and—"

"She has nothing left to hold on to. The thought of you was basically the only thing that kept her going. Your phone calls once a month if we were lucky. Still, hearing your voice always perked her up. Until…"

Despite knowing all too well it would be like this, the blame being piled upon me so quickly and resolutely pierces like a dagger through my heart. My nails bite into my palms as I clench my fists tightly.

"What you did was the final straw. It broke her. And me, for that matter." He quickly wipes away a tear dripping from the corner of his eye.

"What *I* did?" I barely have the energy left to break out in anger.

"Do you have any idea what it does to a parent to have to take that call? To have some stranger tell you that your child, the human being you created, tried to end their life?"

I have no response. I just sit there, tears falling into my beer. Because what can I possibly say to that? I try to think of what Dr. Hakim would say. This is another one of the scenarios we practiced—but I could never fully commit because it was just too damned painful.

I'm so choked up I can't even apologize.

My dad does it for me. "I'm sorry. I'm sorry, Ellie." He holds up his hands. "This is not how I want it to be." His words remind me of the general status of my entire life. "You have to understand… after Nina left, to fill that void, we pinned it all on you. And then you came out… and I know I'm not supposed to say this—I know that very well—but, at the time, it was a blow. One we recovered from quite well. Even brought your mother and I a bit closer together in the end, but you were too far away to notice at that point. Something I don't blame you for. I've had a lot of time to think, Ellie, and I fully realize it must have been hard for you to tell us, this broken family that barely held it together."

Brain fuzzed by an onslaught of tears, I'm amazed by my dad's words. He would never speak like that with my mother in the room. Or, perhaps, I have made a few misdirected assumptions over the years—held on to certain ideas that took on a life of their own in my head.

"But to recover from this." Dad shakes his head in slow, desperate movements. "I don't know."

"I don't want to run anymore." The words tumble from my mouth in hesitant stutters. "It's why I came back."

"I know, sweetheart. I know." Dad knocks back the rest of his beer, signaling Joe for another round. It was a huge mistake to meet him here, in a public place, but Dad seems undeterred by his own tears—and mine.

"I don't even know where to begin." For the first time since arriving, I look him straight in the face. His skin is deeply wrinkled and his breath comes heavy. A sad soul trapped in an unhealthy body.

"How about this—" He pauses as Joe plants another round of beers on our table. "Why don't you invite your new friend Kay over for dinner? I'll make my signature beef stew. It won't just be the three of us." He cocks his head. "Which means your mother will behave." A small smile creeps along his lips, erasing the sadness for an instant.

The unexpected kindness coming from this man I've only seen as sullen and resigned to his gloomy fate in the past twenty years, floors me. For the first time since I was a teenager, I can actually see my dad behind the mask, behind the quiet anger and the endless reproach, mainly expressed by pissing my mother off by staying out at least two hours longer than promised. A man who basically lost two children, but realizes he still has a hint of a chance to make things right.

"I'll ask her tonight." Knowing Kay, she'll probably accept without batting an eyelash. Despite having only just met her again, I'm certain she'll do this for me. "I'll let you know."

"Good." He drains his glass as if its contents are water and he has just spent a week in the desert.

"I—" I'm reluctant to bring this up, but I feel as though I need to tell him. "I e-mailed Nina. I told her what happened."

"That girl…" He makes a weird sniffling noise. "She's just like your mother." Rubbing the back of his hand across his cheek, he glares at me. "Please let me know if she gets in touch."

"I will." I need to stifle the instinct to grab his arm—not something we do in our family.

"Thank you." Unlike yesterday's talk with my mother, this conversation actually feels like progress. Underneath it all, my dad and I seem to have an unspoken kinship, a we're-in-it-together sort of sentiment that connects us at a subconscious level. Even though so many subjects are left untouched, we know we need moments like this to get through it.

"Why did you stay?" *When all your daughters did was run.*

"It was never up to me to leave." His answer comes quick, delivered in a steady, clear voice—as though practiced a million times. "It may be hard for you to see, Ellie, but here —" He taps his chest. "—in our hearts, your mother and I have always meant well." He reaches for a paper napkin stacked at the far end of the table. "We love you girls more than anything." He pauses to blow his nose. "You didn't even say goodbye, Ellie."

I think of the suicide note I left for Sonia to post. I don't remember one word of what was in it. It's safely tucked away in Dr. Hakim's file on me now, after I made it abundantly clear that I never wanted to see it again—that he could shred it for all I cared.

And in my heart, that muscle that kept pumping away beneath my ribs despite me wanting it to stop so desperately,

I know that what I did is not something anyone in my family will ever fully recover from.

We never were like my high school friend Kim's family. When I was invited to dinner with them, I sat flabbergasted by the gentle atmosphere at the table. The kind requests to pass the ketchup. The way her father teased her mother in a playful voice about the dryness of the chicken breasts. Smiles all around the dinner table. Friendly chatter surrounding me. And all I could think was that I must have somehow been teleported to another planet. My family was never like that and it would be foolish to think that could miraculously change now.

I don't say anything because I don't want to refer to *that letter*—written when I had reached the absolute lowest point of my depression.

"Don't worry about your mother. I'll take care of her. I always have."

Instantly, out of habit, a biting, sarcastic comment springs up in my mind, but I drink from my beer until it dissipates into the fog in my brain.

On a basic level, it's actually very simple, Ella. Dr. Hakim's words. *Not one single person on this planet is perfect. Every single one of us is deeply flawed. Either we accept that fact and forgive ourselves for the mistakes we're bound to make, or we let them destroy us.*

But forgiveness is not something that runs in my family.

The door of the bar opens and a group of men my father's age walks in. They raise their hands enthusiastically at him, until they see me. His wounded daughter.

"I'd better go. I'll let you know about dinner."

"You don't have to go because of them, Ellie. Stay. Let's have one more." He's already raising his hand to order the next round. "If anything, I never dreamed I'd be sitting here with you again one day."

"Okay." I nod. Because, for all I've taken from him, I can at least give him this.

Now that his buddies have arrived, our conversation shifts to lighter topics. The cabin. The new mayor. This and that person I haven't seen in years. Because my dad spends most of his time hanging out at The Attic, he knows everything there is to know about everyone in this town.

"Did you know," he leans his torso over the table as best he can, "that Richard Ball's grandson just came out as gay? He told me here two months ago. Wanted to have one of those difficult, drunken talks about it—you know how some men are. They can only show their emotions when they've had a few. But I told him. 'Dickie,' I said, 'he's your grandson. There's nothing to talk about here.'"

13

"Your dad wants to invite me to dinner?" Kay doesn't stop stocking the candy shelves in the shop. "Should I be honored?"

"I really don't know." I'm too mesmerized by the curve of Kay's behind in her jeans when she bends over to unload another box. "Do you need a hand with that?"

"Sure. If you could just pass these to me. All this bending at my age." She straightens her posture before arching her back.

I walk over to her and we stand staring at each other for an instant.

"Wouldn't miss it, by the way." Another wink—this one goes straight to my gut. "When is it and am I expected to dress up?"

"God no. Although I am curious to see you in a dress."

"If you want to see me in a dress, you'll have to buy me one. The last time I wore one was at my prom, so I guess you'd have to be my date as well. I don't put out for anything less."

"Let's save that for a different occasion then. Wouldn't

want to waste that on dinner with the Goodmans." I squat next to Kay—my eyes level with the golden-brown skin of her thighs—and start handing her packets of brightly colored gummy bears.

"Dream on, Little Ella." She smiles down at me. "About the dress, I mean. A date can be discussed." She takes a few packets from me and her finger brushes against the back of my hand. The touch sizzles through me as if administered on an entirely different part of my body. My libido, which pretty much disappeared as my thoughts of despair increased, seems to have found a new lease on life as well.

"I guess I'll have to hold you to that." I flirt without thinking about the repercussions and, for a brief instant, it feels so good I forget to be careful. "I may even cook you a meal." The box is empty and I push myself up.

"Oh really? And what would that be? A soufflé of break-fast bars?"

I chuckle. "I have a few signature dishes I may surprise you with."

"It's a deal then. Tomorrow I'll have dinner with your family and this weekend you'll cook for me. If you ask me, the order of events is slightly reversed, but I can improvise. I'm easy like that."

"Thank you." I all but bow reverently. "Really."

"Don't mention it." There's so much more lurking behind Kay's words and it hits me that failure to communi-cate—to express what's really going on—is one of the issues that put me in this situation.

"We should probably talk."

Kay quirks up one eyebrow. "We should?"

"Yes." Nervously, I pick up the empty box and start folding it in on itself.

"Let me do that. You science geeks are not the most

practical of people." She tugs the box from my hands and with a few compact, swift movements flattens it completely.

"You'd better not offend me *before* I cook for you."

"I'll do my best." She disposes of the box in a small container next to the counter. "Why don't you come inside so we can talk."

I follow Kay into the lodge where, without asking, she pours me a whiskey. We huddle around the kitchen table, nothing but silence around us—and the thumping of my heart.

I take a sip from my drink before starting the conversation. "Look, Kay, I really enjoy your company. I think you know that." I'm surprised at how easy the words come. "But—"

"It's all right, Ella. You don't have to say it. I think I know." Is that disappointment in her tone? A sort of unsettledness I haven't heard before?

"No." I shake my head firmly. "I need to say it."

"Okay." Her glance has gone vacant. The guarded stare of a woman who has been hurt one too many times.

"I like you. I mean, I really really like you." My earlier found eloquence is already starting to elude me. "If the circumstances were different, we would have gone on a date already, but, uh, I need you to understand that romance—or anything resembling romance…" My cheeks start burning brightly. "That's not something I can deal with right now. It's a distraction. An easy way out. A cop out." I repeat the words I spoke to my dad earlier. "I didn't come here to fall in love."

Kay doesn't speak for a few moments, just stares into her glass. "As much as I appreciate your candor, I think you're getting ahead of yourself a bit here."

"Oh." Did I read this situation wrong? Were we not just flirting heavily in the shop?

"I don't mean I'm not attracted to you. I think you know that I am, being the heart-on-my-sleeve kind of person that I am. Shit. I've barely left the West Waters grounds since you arrived. It's not really my habit to look in on guests several times a day. Or to go skinny dipping with them at midnight." Kay fixes her gaze on me. "Just now, you invited me to dinner with your parents. For moral support, I presume. Which implies you trust me on a very primal level. You have done so from the beginning. You opened up to me and I don't suspect you do that with many people you just ran into again after twenty years of absence. So, I guess what I'm asking is why would you think you wouldn't be able to trust me with this? With us? Do you really think I would let you fall in love and forget about why you came here in the first place? That I would ever allow you to see me as a mere distraction?" There's genuine hurt in Kay's voice.

"I'm sorry. I didn't mean to imply anything. I just, for once in my life, wanted to be absolutely honest." I shove the whiskey aside. It's too strong—just like the memories that cling to it after the last one I drank. "I guess you have to know what I'm like to fully understand. Back in Boston, losing myself in a new relationship was my favorite means of escape. The thrill of the chase. Those exhilarating first months. Peaking dopamine levels that made me forget about myself. A temporary fix. Until that moment came when I realized I had fallen for someone for all the wrong reasons— again." I barely have the nerve to glance at Kay. "I really can't afford that to happen here. Not now, when I'm this fragile. I'm not strong enough."

"No date then?" A kind smirk has found its way to Kay's lips. My heart leaps at the sight of it.

"I'll cook for you anyway. I feel as if I have something to prove now." I reach out my hand across the table, eager for Kay's touch.

"You don't have to prove anything to me, Ella." To my relief, Kay covers my hand with her palm. "Just tell me this." A sadness has crept into her gaze again, but there's tenderness, too—and understanding. "Are you glad to be alive?"

"Yes," I say without hesitation.

Kay squeezes her fingers tighter around my hand. "Then don't write this off just yet."

I shake my head, too fraught with emotion to speak. Kay lifts my hand off the table and cups it in both of hers. "And I will come to dinner with Dee and John." Her thumb runs across my palm. "Unless you think it's a distraction."

I get the point she's trying to make loud and clear. I also see that Kay is nothing like Thalia or any of the women who came before her. Those women whose only mistake was to fall for someone as lost as me.

"Thank you." It's all I can say.

"*Quid pro quo*, Little Ella." The touch of Kay's fingers is starting to produce a familiar heat in my blood. "I'll go with you tomorrow if you stop apologizing and thanking me for nothing."

A giggle escapes me, but we both know that what Kay is doing for me—not just accompanying me to dinner with my parents, but simply being her patient, good-natured, wise self —is not nothing. She's saving me.

14

I can tell by the look on my mother's face—tight smile, dismissive glint in her eyes—that she's not particularly happy with Kay's presence. But for me, it changes everything. Kay's an easy conversationalist, sucking at least half the tension that always hangs heavy at my parents' house out of the air.

"I'll never forget that time when Patrick serenaded Mabel at the bonfire." My dad, on the other hand, is going out of his way to make Kay feel welcome. I don't even want to think about the conversation he and my mother must have had when he announced she'd be joining us for dinner. "Now that was true love if ever I saw it."

"And he could barely hold a tune." Kay is her relaxed, unassuming self. "Unfortunately, I inherited his singing voice. But at least I don't make a fool of myself that easily." She dressed up in jeans and a glittery spaghetti strap top I would never have pictured her in, but it suits her so well—brings out the sparkle in her eyes. I realize that, with Kay here, I feel as close to relaxed as I can ever remember being in this house.

Dad and Kay both chuckle, while Mom and I still shuffle nervously in our seats.

"Shall we eat?" Mom asks. "Your father has been slaving away in the kitchen all day."

"A hobby I picked up after retiring." Dad addresses Kay again. I'm beginning to think he invited her more for his own sake than mine.

"Otherwise he'd be spending *all* his time at The Attic," Mom cuts in again, that typical edge to her voice. She was never good at cracking jokes, always needing to convey some hard truth in them, or at least put Dad down in the process.

"You won't hear me complain about that either." Kay's the first to rise.

"I've been meaning to talk to you about my open tab. Is there no special discount for loyal customers?" Dad gets up as well and practically elbows Kay in the biceps.

"I just own the place. I don't interfere with management, John. Otherwise half the town would be asking me what you just had the audacity to suggest." She shoots Dad a smile. "Can't wait to taste your stew."

We gather around the table and I sit next to Kay, her presence like a shield around me. Dad serves us while Mom pours more wine. My eyes linger on her own more than generous helping.

"This is truly delicious, John." Kay turns to face me. "You have big shoes to fill." With Kay at the table with us, it almost feels as if I'm part of an every day all-American family. Not without its secrets and painful memories—just like any other family—but at least capable of normal, stress-free dinner chatter. "Ella promised to prepare me a feast this weekend." Kay stares both my parents in the face without qualms, as if there's no place she'd rather be, but I can't imagine she's actually enjoying this. "I bet you're quite the cook as well, Dee?"

"Mom's an excellent baker. What did you make for dessert?" I ask my mother, who has barely touched her food and is, in my opinion, much too focused on that giant glass of wine looming in front of her.

"Just an apple tart. I was feeling a bit off this afternoon. Not enough energy to spend much time in the kitchen. Besides, when your dad's in there, there's no room for me." When I glare at my mother's face, it's like looking into a fast-forward mirror. Is this me in twenty-five years? An existence depleted of all joy. A marriage of, I guess after all these years, convenience to someone I can't bother to show respect for, least of all in public. At least I won't have children for whom it's too difficult to come home more than every few years, or, in Nina's case, ever.

"Having health issues?" Kay is kind enough to ask. She doesn't know that my mother suffers from most ailments known and unknown to mankind, albeit not always substantiated by blood work or a doctor's diagnosis. Funnily enough, most of my mother's health problems started cropping up just after she found out about my dad's affair.

Mom shakes her head in defeat. "I'm an old woman. It's been all downhill for a while now." She drinks some more. I don't really want to think about it, but I know exactly where this evening is going. I try to exchange a glance with my father, but he stares at something on the opposite wall with an empty look in his eyes.

"Not everyone gets the chance to live past their retirement age," Kay says, an unfamiliar hint of hardness in her tone.

"While that is unmistakably true, clearly, not everyone wants to, either." My mother's obvious jab at me hits me straight in the gut.

My dad slams his fist on the table. "The only daughter we're on regular speaking terms with is sitting right in front of us. She's here. With us. You can at least try to be happy about that, Dee."

"Happy?" Mom gives a disdainful huff. "What a joke."

You are not responsible for anyone else's happiness. I focus on Dr. Hakim's words—the ones I clung to the most.

Under the table, I feel Kay's hand on my knee. I gather strength from her touch, despite the rage building in my gut.

"Dad's right. I'm sitting right here, Mom. Whatever you need to say to me, you can say it." I realize I've barely spoken all night. My voice feels tight and unused, my throat swollen.

"I can't." Mom shakes her head in despair. "What if I say something that makes you try again?"

Kay digs her fingertips into the flesh around my knee.

"That's not going to happen. I'm not the same person I was before." Instinctively, I shuffle closer to Kay. "Also, Mom, what I did had nothing to do with what you might have said or done. Nothing. It was me and only me."

Dad fumbles with his napkin, pushing it against his wet cheeks. Mom's head hangs low, as if her body has given up already. Next to me, Kay sits with a straight back, the expression on her face not giving away much.

"I came back," I continue, "because this family is as broken as I am. Because we all need to heal. Not to assign blame, but because this is where my life started. This is where I grew up. You're my parents and, well, we may not get along as well as we'd like, but what I did was not your fault. I've been depressed for a long time and my mistakes are my own."

"Was it a mistake, Ellie?" Dad's voice crackles. "Or did you really want to die?"

I can't reply to that. Not even Dr. Hakim has asked me that question and gotten anything resembling an answer to it. I certainly didn't want to live anymore. Is that the same as wanting to die? Or is there nuance in everything?

I suppose, in the end, I couldn't care less if I lived or died. Except that every minute I had to drag myself through my sad existence was one minute too many. Every day I had to go through life with a brain that constantly questioned even the smallest decisions was one day too many. But what weighed on me most of all was how the imbalance in my brain chemistry had me convinced that, despite short bursts of happiness—which were possibly only so vivid and joyful because of the contrast with the utter bleakness of any other day—the future was always, unquestionably, black.

I did want to die. But I lived.

"Maybe we should call it a night." Kay stands up and curves an arm around my neck. "Maybe that's enough for now."

"It's just that, Ellie," my father doesn't stop, "your mother and I live in constant fear that you'll, uh, do it again."

Has this brought them closer together as well? I'm not used to either of them making a statement for both of them as a couple. I want to get up, but I'm afraid my legs will fail. Both Kay's hands rest on my shoulders and she squeezes the tight muscles there softly. I try to visualize Dr. Hakim's solemn face. The response we came up with—*I* came up with after long minutes of silence from him—sits too far back in my brain, in that obscured place I can never reach under pressure. *They would never say something like that*, I had assured Dr. Hakim. *Never in a million years. My family doesn't say things out loud. We prefer to imply things wordlessly—not enough room for misunderstanding and frustration otherwise.*

His reply: *They may surprise you. Traumatic events change people. Makes them say and do unexpected things.*

So far, Dr. Hakim has been proven right many more times than I care to count.

"I won't try again." It's easy enough to say with Kay

gently massaging my shoulders—and I know it's the exact reason why I can't get romantically involved with her. Not now. "I'm getting better. Working hard at it." These are not the words I'm supposed to say, but they're all I've got. A stop gap. A quick reassurance, like my mother used to give Nina and me after we'd taken a clumsy fall that had shocked us more than hurt us. *Stop crying and it will all be over in a few seconds.* She was usually right, but this hardly compares. "I know it's not easy, but you're going to have to trust me. There's no other way."

I imagine my mother having to triple her dosage of sleeping pills to get any sleep at all. She shouldn't even be drinking with all the medicine she swallows on a daily basis. A few years ago, when staying with them over the holidays, I checked her medicine cabinet—the one in the bathroom she stocks for daily, frequent use. I found Valium, Xanax, Prozac. The works. And to think she scolds my dad for drinking too much.

"Okay." My father pushes his chair back and, to my amazement, puts his hand on my mother's shoulder. The only time I can remember them touching is when my mother prodded him in the arm violently when he was snoring so loudly she couldn't hear the TV. "We trust you, Ellie."

Mom is crying now, short, sniffling sounds from her mouth and nose, but it's not what takes me aback the most. What baffles me more than anything is that she accepts my dad's display of affection and puts her hand on his.

"It's not easy getting through this," she says through her tears, curling her fingers tightly around Dad's hand.

"I know. I'm sorry." Kay's fingers dig deep into my flesh, but she can't stop me from apologizing because, for this, I will always be sorry.

"Do you want to stay?" Kay asks in a barely audible whisper.

I shake my head. Perhaps I should stay, but this is enough for one night. My ability to think clearly and objectively always seems to shrink whenever I set foot in this house, but now it's also muddled by sadness and lessened by this sight of my parents' version of a tender embrace which, quite frankly, touches me more than anything has the past few years.

"I'm going now." I inhale deeply, but, still unsure about the capability of my legs to carry me, don't get up.

"Let me get you some apple tart to go." Mom drops Dad's hand and straightens her posture.

"No, Mom." I try to look her in the eyes, but end up glancing at the light switch on the wall behind her head. "Why don't you bring some to the cabin tomorrow?"

Slowly, my mother nods while my invitation sinks in.

15

"Whiskey?" Kay asks after she has parked the car.

"How about a swim instead?" I look at her face under the dim pale-yellow light of the West Waters parking lot.

"Clothing optional?" she counters.

"Somehow, for me, wearing a bathing suit after dark is no longer an option." A timid smile breaks on my face, cutting through the sadness that has been with me all night. "You've ruined me forever."

"Ruined? Freed, you mean." A low giggle bubbles up from Kay's throat. "You city girls. Tsk." She shakes her head in mock disdain. "I can teach you a thing or two."

"No doubt there." It's cozy in the darkness of the car. Intimate. Just the two of us in a closed space, the AC gently humming, Kay's hands still on the steering wheel.

"Come on, Little Ella." She cocks her head a little, drawing her lips into a grin—probably as a stand-in apology for still calling me by my childhood nickname. "Let's wash away those tears."

When we get out of the car and walk toward the lake,

Kay grabs my hand. It feels comforting and disturbing at the same time, but, if I'm certain of only one thing, it's that Kay's intentions are good.

"How are you feeling?" We stand at the edge of the water for a second, facing each other, my hand still in hers.

"Emotionally stripped bare, I guess." I have no problem looking Kay straight in the eyes. "The cruel thing about surviving is that you have to face the hurt you caused your loved-ones head on."

"I said you were brave. You could have chosen not to come. To hide away in Boston. To continue the trend of not speaking to your parents. But, instead, you came home." When she smiles, Kay's teeth glint in the weak moonlight. "I, for one, am very happy you opted to return to Northville."

With every fiber of my being I fight the urge to kiss her. Even though I know that with Kay it's not like it was with Thalia, and Myriam before her, and Christine prior to that. Kay is not a diversion. She's part of my quest for truth. She sees me in a way no one has before. Not only because I'm a new person, but even more so because she's the first woman I've allowed to look so deep into my wounded, flawed soul.

Still, I can't kiss her. Just being around her already feels too good. Being under strict instructions, I can't thank her anymore than I already have, either.

"Come on." Ending the moment, Kay drops my hand and pulls her sparkly top over her head.

When Kay stands in front of me in jeans and bra, my heartbeat pulses in body parts I haven't been aware of for a long time. Quickly, I turn away and undress, trying to ignore the fact that getting naked with her in the dark is probably not the best idea. I jump into the water as fast as I can, not looking behind me once I'm in. With swift strokes, I swim to the middle, the balmy water of the lake immediately soothing.

But, as Kay swims toward me, the throbbing recommences. Perhaps it's my raw emotional state that has heightened my senses. Or the memory of Kay's hand on my knee when I needed it most. If she comes too close now, or says something encouraging and flattering again, I'm not sure I'll be able to stop myself.

"Don't take this the wrong way, please." We're both treading water about two feet away from each other. "But I'm going to swim away and not come back."

"Ever?" Kay quirks up one eyebrow, pulling her entire face into a comical expression.

The surface of the water around me trembles as I chuckle. *As if I could ever stay away from her.* Lips pursed into a pout, I shake my head.

"Do what you need to do, but remember that your key is in your purse and your purse is over there." She points her thumb to the spot outside the lodge where we jumped in. "And I haven't unlocked the house yet, so there are no towels outside. Unless you don't mind walking to your cabin dripping wet and stark naked." She has dipped so low under water her chin rises in and out as she speaks. "And Uncle Pete may have a heart attack when he encounters a nude female in the dark."

"I guess I didn't really think it through."

"Go have a swim and cool off. I'll get out and leave a towel by your clothes."

"No, really. You don't have to get out for my sake."

"I live here. I have access to this lake all year round."

"But soon it'll be too cold and—"

"What are we bickering about exactly?"

"I may have forgotten." I haven't though. Under water, my nipples are rock hard and my skin has broken out in goose bumps.

"If you need space, you've got it. You're going through a lot at the moment. I have no problem understanding that."

"It's just that, uh, I'm not sure I have the energy to fight this. God knows I don't want to, either."

"I bet it would help if you were to put out of your head that this absolutely can't happen."

"A little reverse psychology?"

"Call it what you like." From her tone, I can only derive that Kay wants to kiss me as much as I want to kiss her.

"I'm scared, Kay. Having you around is the best thing that has happened to me in a long time. There are a lot of things to consider."

"You think too much, that's your main problem." Kay moves a little closer. "But consider this. I'm not usually someone who shies away from making the first move, but with you, I feel as though I have to make an exception. Ball's in your court."

The mere fact that we're having this conversation not even an hour after leaving my parents' house, is reason enough to listen to my brain instead of my heart. Because, in this very moment, Kay *is* an escape route. On the other hand, it beats sitting alone in the cabin feeling sorry for myself.

"You're doing it again."

"What?"

"Overthinking it."

"You don't understand—"

"I do, Ella. I do understand." She lets herself drift away from me in the water. "You need more time. I can see that. If, in your overused, tired mind, kissing me equals an abrupt stop to your healing process, then you shouldn't do it. If, on the other hand, you could come to understand that allowing your feelings—your impulses and your reflexes—to guide you again, is just another step toward a less broken version of yourself, then, I guess, you should think about trying it." She floats away further. "I'm going to get us some towels now."

I watch her swim away. She makes it to the landing within a few minutes—minutes during which I can't seem to move—and hoists herself out of the water elegantly. And I can't tear my eyes away from her even if I wanted to. She crouches down to look for her keys in her jeans pocket and, naked and dripping, walks toward the back door of the lodge.

We've only just got reacquainted, yet it's as though I've known her forever. Before I can change my mind, I swim to the edge and, just as Kay returns, wrapped in a plush white towel, an extra one rolled up under her arm for me, I push myself out of the water. I notice how her glance lingers on my body, how all movement of her muscles momentarily stops.

"Here's your towel," Kay mumbles.

"Forget the towel." I step closer, pull her toward me, close my eyes and kiss her. The earth doesn't stop turning, but my head does spin. Because, in the pit of my stomach, I feel that this kiss is the beginning of something I already know I will never be able to live without.

When Kay grabs the back of my head with one hand, the touch of her fingertips travels through my system with tingling pangs. When we come up for air and our eyes meet, any thought of what should or should not happen has fled my brain.

"What does it feel like?" she asks, her voice low and husky. "To stop worrying and give yourself the time and space to enjoy the moment?"

"Fucking hot." I barely recognize my own voice. I'm still naked, every nerve-ending in my body pulsing with that old, forgotten ache.

"Come here." Kay unrolls the second towel and brings it

behind my back, tugging me closer toward her with it. "I'm all for a bit of indecent exposure, but there are limits to everything." She casts one last, longing glance across the front of my body before tucking a corner of the towel underneath the hem of the other end.

"*You* come here." I lift my arms to pull her closer again, undoing her efforts as it makes the towel slide right off me, exposing my tortured nipples to the breezy night air. Neither one of us cares about indecent exposure anymore as our lips lock and our tongues explore each other's mouth in another moment I will never forget.

I want her hands on my breasts. I want to tug the towel from her body so our skin can collide, but it's simply not in my nature to discard all rational thought so quickly, and I know that a kiss is as far as this can go for now. That doesn't mean we have to stop kissing though.

Our lips crash together again and again, under the moonlight reflecting off the surface of the water, at the edge of this lake that is so intertwined with Kay's entire being, I fall in love with it a little bit too.

"God, you're beautiful," I whisper in between deep, exploring kisses.

Kay emits a groan before speaking. "We have to stop now." She doesn't say it with a lot of conviction, but I know she's right. I have my natural tendency to respect strict boundaries to call upon, but for someone who is, in many ways, the exact opposite of me, this lesson in self-restraint can't be easy. Kay finds my ear and whispers, "The things I want to do to you." It's almost enough to pierce right through my armor of self-consciousness.

"I'll have that whiskey now." I step away from her—it's the least I can do after all she's done for me—and pick up my towel, fastening it securely around my torso.

"Perhaps a cold shower, too." Kay flashes me a pained

grin and it's as if I can see what kind of lover she is in the way she glances at me in that moment. Even with her patience tested, she would go the extra mile—for me.

Perhaps, as a safety measure, I should go back to my own cabin, but I simply can't imagine—can't even bear to think of —myself alone tonight. So, I follow Kay inside, gladly accept the robe and glass of whiskey she hands me, and sit with her in silence for a while—until we both come back to our senses enough to resume conversation.

A different dimension has opened up between us. A fence has been torn down, lifting us to a higher level of intimacy. I want to know so many more details about her life. After all, I've stripped myself bare for her, shown her what's inside my soul as best I could.

"And we haven't even gone on that date yet," Kay says, her eyes peering at me over the rim of her glass.

"Seeing as we're doing so many things in random order, I'll still cook for you." Suddenly exhausted, I relax against my chair and decide to leave the more probing questions for date night.

"You could serve me warmed up grass from the lawn outside your cabin and I'd still think it delicious, as long as you kiss me after." The longing in Kay's glance doesn't seem to subside, even her voice is drenched in it. I can't help but think of all the love I squandered by deeming myself not worthy of it. Of all the pointless fights I picked to drive away women who genuinely cared for me so I could, once again, prove the eternal hypothesis—the one claiming at least half of my brain activity at all times: why would anyone in their right mind love someone as dysfunctional, as imperfectly put-together, as me?

"Good to know." I want to scoot my chair closer, feel the warmth of her skin against mine. "At least dessert will be halfway decent."

"Do you want me there?" A more serious expression descends on Kay's features. "When your mom comes over tomorrow?"

I do. God, I do. "I think I need to face this one alone." Also, now that we've kissed, a reluctance to let her see me like that again, at my uttermost vulnerable, has started to crop up.

"I'll be around if you need me." Kay extends her leg and lets her foot glide over my shin.

"Can I stay here tonight? In your guest room, I mean." The touch of her skin against mine starts off another round of deep throbbing in my flesh.

"Yes and no." She catches my leg between her ankles. "You can stay but not in the guest room."

"Look, Kay," I start. "I'm not sure—"

"I want you in my bed, Ella. Nothing will happen, I can guarantee you that, but I want you in my bed." She leans her elbows on her thighs, bringing her face closer to mine. "I don't need much, but I need that."

I'm desperate to do something for her for a change, so I nod determinedly. "Okay."

"Best lay off the booze then." She cracks a smile.

In response, I empty my glass and stifle a yawn.

"You must be tired." She deposits her own empty glass on the table. "We haven't even talked about what was said at dinner. We can if you want to."

"You're not my shrink, Kay. Just being here with you is enough." Should I email Dr. Hakim about this development? What if he advises me to break it off?

"Okay." She bends her knees, retracting her legs from where they were resting around my ankle, and gets up. "Come on. I'll get you a sexy nighty."

In her bedroom, we slip out of our robes and into oversized, faded t-shirts, our backs chastely turned to one another.

Sliding under the covers takes me back to the very first time I became truly aware of my attraction toward girls. I was fifteen and staying over at Sally McMullen's house. Not having a clue as to why I was so uneasy in her bed, I lay stiffly by her side all night, not sleeping a wink until at dawn, exhausted, I fell asleep on her shoulder, waking up a few hours later so mortified I couldn't speak to her for weeks after.

"I'm a light sleeper, so if you need anything during the night, just give me a shake. A gentle one will do." Kay flips off the light and lies on her back. The room is dark enough to strip me of my nerves. The heat of her body radiating on my side. The presence of another human being in the same bed. The memory of the kiss. Instead of arousing me more, it calms me and, already, I can feel my eyelids closing.

"Good night, Kay," I mumble.

"Are you falling asleep already?"

"I'm so tired." Too tired to analyze what the tone of her voice means.

"Turn on your side."

As if we've been sleeping in the same bed for years, I turn to face the wall and, seconds later, I feel Kay's strong arm wrapping around me, her soft breasts against my back, and her breath on the back of my neck. Only extreme emotional fatigue keeps me from bursting into spontaneous tears at the kindness of her gesture.

16

I wake up alone in Kay's bed. The room is flooded with light and when my eyes find the alarm clock, I realize I haven't slept like this in months—maybe years. I can smell bacon and another realization hits me: I haven't felt this cared for in a long time. Perhaps because I didn't let myself, but with Kay, it's all so effortless. I can't stop questioning my motives—questioning even the smallest events in life has been my main occupation for as long as I can remember—but for a few seconds while stretching my limbs before pushing my nose into Kay's pillow and inhaling her scent, I allow myself to forget why I'm here, and revel in the prospect of this brand new day.

Then I remember that my mother is visiting this afternoon. And that I'm supposed to prepare a fancy meal for Kay tonight. A stark contrast to how lazily I've spent my days so far at West Waters. Before I let today's to-do list overwhelm me, I scan Kay's room. No closet. No drawers. Just a king-size bed with a night stand on either side and a large mirror on the wall facing the bed. Sober would probably be the best way to describe her room, or, perhaps, designed for only a few well-defined purposes. At that thought, the memory of last night's kiss floods my brain. Kay's lips. Her smell. The tingle in my stomach. The pulsing between my legs. My head is filled with only Kay and the possibilities of our date tonight.

A knock on the door pulls me from my reverie.

"Morning Snorky," Kay says, her hair still disheveled. She's wearing the same t-shirt she wore to bed.

"Really?" Our first night in bed together and I kept her awake with my snoring?

"Just kidding. It was more of a gentle purr." She brings in a tray with two plates heaped with eggs and bacon. "Are you hungry?"

"Always when you cook." I take the tray from her, the delicious smell of another breakfast prepared by Kay making my mouth water.

"Coffee?"

"Yes, please."

"Coming right up." As Kay darts out of the bedroom, I wonder if I've somehow landed myself in the plot of the most romantic movie ever made, whether I'm still dreaming or I really did wake up in this magnificent woman's bed.

Before I have a chance to pinch myself, Kay heads back into the room with two steaming mugs.

We install ourselves cross-legged on the bed, the tray between us, the coffee mugs safely deposited on the night stands.

"I slept like a log," I say before popping a piece of bacon in my mouth.

"Glad to know I have such an exhilarating effect on you." Kay raises her eyebrows.

"Did you sleep well?" I try to ignore Kay's remark, not really knowing what to say.

"Honestly? No. Perhaps it wasn't the best idea to invite

you into my bed after kissing you while you were naked. Difficult image to get out of my head, you know?" She smirks. "But hey, I asked for it." There's a twinkle in Kay's eyes. What are we waiting for? A note from my doctor? A permission slip from my conscience? I want her and, clearly, she wants me.

"No pressure, Ella. I'm attracted to you, but I have no expectations. I'm not some chick you need to put out for to keep interested." Kay's voice has gone all serious.

Again, I'm torn between the two extremes that seem to make up my emotional life. As much as I love having breakfast in bed with Kay, I can't take her words at face value. I'm sure she means them—now—but she's only witnessed about ten percent of my personality—and only the well-behaved side. After every failed attempt at building a healthy relationship, I stared at my reflection in the mirror, alone and heartbroken, and I knew for a fact that I wasn't worth it. That I couldn't do it. That once a woman got close enough to discover the real me beneath the shiny veneer that comes with a brand new love affair, she had every right to run.

"Ella?" Kay nudges my shin with her toe.

"Sorry." I stack some eggs on my fork.

"Where did you go just now?"

The magic of the moment, of this beautiful morning with Kay, has disappeared. Another conflict pops up in my brain. Am I really trying to woo another woman by confiding my blackest secrets to her? And what does that make her? Instead of enjoying Kay's company, of simply eating her food and engaging in some carefree banter, I've ruined it—again. Instead of Doctor of Biology, my business card should say: Ella Goodman, Ruiner of Romance.

The only way to go is right through it. One of Dr. Hakim's quotes stored in my phone. *If you want to heal, there's no way back.*

"You have no idea how much I wish I could just jump into this headfirst." I can barely look at Kay, because, after the kiss, I see her differently. "But that's no longer an option for me."

"As long as you don't run away from me for all the wrong reasons." Kay pops a piece of bacon in her mouth, chews it unceremoniously.

But my usual M.O. of crash and burn is all I know. I have no idea how to play this slow game. It doesn't help that Kay looks at me with that glint of desire in her eyes.

"I guess I'm just nervous about Mom's visit." It's not a lie, but it's not the whole truth either.

"I'll be here for you afterwards." Kay presses her toe into my leg again. "And if you're too torn up after her visit, it's an excellent excuse to get out of cooking for me." A smile flits along her lips.

"Why do you want this, Kay?" I have no idea where I get the courage to ask that question, unless it's just more self-sabotage: question it to death before it can grow into anything substantial. "Do you get a kick out of trying to save lost causes? Does it turn you on that I'm so broken?"

Kay's fork clatters against her near-empty plate. "First of all, stop referring to yourself as a lost cause. Second, that feeling-sorry-for-yourself schtick doesn't work on me, so you might as well put a sock in it now." There's not a hint of anger in her tone. Nothing I can latch on to, because anger is what I grew up with. Anger, my very own blueprint for love.

I'm not allowed to apologize, so instead I shovel some eggs into my mouth. They taste divine. Kay is divine. Over my plate, I stare at her legs, her strong thighs disappearing into a pair of boxer shorts. Everything about her is magnificent and, like that one mosquito in the night that never gives up, the thought keeps hammering in my mind: what am I bringing to the table? How can this ever be a meeting of equals?

"Go for a swim. It'll make you feel better. Clear your head," she says.

"After a breakfast like this, all I want to do is go back to sleep."

"Don't you have to go shopping?" The smile is back on Kay's face. "To prepare me some fancy city-style food."

17

Waiting for my mother at the cabin feels like a do-over of our failed attempt a few days ago. Only, this time, Kay won't come to my rescue before we have a chance to say anything of meaning.

I sit on the porch and hear her footsteps approach. Small, clipped steps walking purposefully toward me on the graveled path.

When my friend Trish had her first baby five years ago, she told me that the love she felt for little Josie was so obliterating she couldn't compare it to anything else. I remember wondering if that was a universal feeling among new mothers around the world—if my own mother ever felt that way about Nina and me.

After my mom has deposited her pie in the kitchen, she grabs me by the shoulders, turns me toward her, and hugs me so tightly I fear she may crack one of my ribs. When we let loose, we both have tears in our eyes.

"Do you have anything stronger than coffee?" she asks.

I arch up my eyebrows, unsure this is the best way to start a coffee date.

"Just the one, to take the edge off. I know we have some serious business to discuss and the pie is just dress-up."

I'm not used to my mother being so forthright. Taken aback, I head for the fridge and dig up the bottle of white wine I had planned on serving Kay tonight. I pour us both a modest glass and put the bottle back.

"I'm glad we never sold this place," Mom says after we've installed ourselves on the porch, both of us looking out over the lake. "Although I came this close." She brings her thumb and index finger together, only leaving half an inch between them. "He brought her here. To this place where we vacationed with you and Nina, our girls."

Although Dad's affair hung over our lives like a dark cloud, after the big confessional moment, it was never directly talked about again, despite silently dominating almost every conversation in the Goodman house. Again, Mom surprises me with her forwardness.

"Are you kidding me?" I need to take a sip from my wine to process.

Mom shakes her head, but not in her usual victim-like way. "That's how I found out. She left a pair of tights under the bed. How cliché is that, Ella?" To my utter amazement, she even manages a chuckle. Who is this woman sitting next to me? She looks like Dee Goodman, but seems possessed by someone else's spirit. She takes a big gulp of her wine. "I have a confession to make." She twirls the stem of her glass between her fingers. "Your father and I contacted your doctor in Boston this morning. Not to check up on you, just to ask for guidance on how to, uh, handle this."

"You did what?" Pure rage flares in the pit of my stomach, quickly making its way up. It's so typical that she would go behind my back.

"I should have asked first. I know that. And, for the record, your father was against it, but I needed to do something. I couldn't risk coming here again and not being able to find a crack in this wall between us. It's been killing me. I'm so scared, Ella. So scared of losing you forever."

"You had no right." My anger diminishes at the sight of her tears. It reminds me of an article I read on parenting not so long ago. *Never let your children see you cry or fight. Be strong for them. Resolve your conflicts behind closed doors.* For all the times I've witnessed my parents' passive-aggressive argument routine, I've hardly ever seen my mom cry.

"I know. I know I had no right to, but I'm glad I called." She fishes for a handkerchief in her purse. "We have so much to talk about. So much time to catch up on. I'm your mother, Ella. I wanted to do it right for once." And just like that, my mother's eternal problem rises to the surface once again: good intentions, flawed execution.

"What did he say?" It feels a bit like asking how things went after my mother went to a parents-teachers night when I was still in school.

"He sounded like a lovely man." Mom pauses to blow her nose and wipe away most of the tears. "He seemed to understand why I called, put me at ease. Advised me to 'listen without blinkers on'. Obviously, he was quite reluctant to engage in conversation about you directly, but just having the opportunity to talk to him for a few minutes was enough for me." Another tear sits at the ready in the corner of her eye. "Ever since *that call*, every minute of my life has been consumed with worry." A tear falls down her cheek. "But I'm here for you. I'm here to listen. I don't want you to hold back, not on my account."

I drain the rest of my glass, desperate for some sort of buzz to make this awkward moment more bearable. I have dreamed of an opportunity like this many a time, but every time the scenario played out in my head, it ended with yelling followed by more hurt feelings and misunderstanding

—like any Friday evening at our house when I was a teenager. Now, it feels more as if I've landed in the middle of a very uncomfortable nightmare.

"I guess the reason why I haven't been coming home as much as you'd like," I start, gazing over the water, the possibility of having to meet my mother's eyes keeping my neck stiff and immobile, "is because… there's no joy. There's no love in that house." I feel my mother stir next to me, but she manages to hold her tongue. "If there is, it's a very twisted, very conditional, very stifling kind." I try to block out the voices in my head and continue. "I came back now because, under Dr. Hakim's guidance, I've concluded that to accept myself, I need to accept where I came from. I need to make some sort of peace. I need to feel that there's something more between us than a very, very loose family tie." My thumb and ring finger tap against each other in a nervous fashion.

"I mean, I know you and Dad love me, and I love you too. You're my parents, my family. But something has gone so wrong between us, I can't even put it into words. And, the worst thing is, before, uh, what I did, I had come to accept it was just one of those things. Sometimes children fall out with their parents. When the past has been too toxic, when too much has been said or done, or perhaps, in our case, silently implied.

"But the way you and Dad treated each other has left its mark on me. And, by no means am I here to fix your marriage, I'm here to fix myself. To ask a few difficult questions and to get some answers." The words roll out of me, leaving me breathless. I'm not even sure of all the things I just said, mostly because I can't believe I said them.

"Ask away." In those two words, I hear how broken my mother is. I don't need to look at her to see her slumped posture and troubled gaze.

"I asked you the same question many years ago, and you brushed it off as though it was just a silly child's thought." I turn to look at her. "If he made you so unhappy, why did you stay?"

"Oh, Ella. I can see why, to you and your sister, it might have seemed like the wrong decision, but you don't know what your father has done for me." Tears streak her cheeks. "You and I, we are much more alike than you know."

"You're my mother. Of course we have a lot in common."

"I've never resorted to what you—" She hesitates. "I've been in your situation. I know how you feel, Ella, more than you'll ever know. I know what that darkness does to you."

It doesn't really come as a shock, but to hear her say the words still surprises me. When Dr. Hakim asked me if depression ran in my family, I was never able to give him a straight answer.

"A year after Nina was born, I spent four months in Stewart Center in Portland. It was the hardest thing I ever did, leaving my baby to get better. It helped, but it's been a struggle ever since." She eyes her empty wine glass longingly, but I don't get up. "Your father was by my side through everything. How hypocritical would it have been to leave him because of that affair? We had so many other considerations. You girls. My illness." In desperation, she throws her hands in the air. "Was it the right decision in the end? I believe that for your father and me it was. You haven't been around for a while, Ella. We're good now."

"But…" I'm not sure if I have the right to ask after what my mother just admitted to. "What about the endless fighting? The constant disparaging tone you used with him? The complete lack of respect?" I try to keep my voice steady, try not to show the anger I always carry with me quietly.

My mother sucks in a deep breath, her shoulders sagging

again. "I guess that, back then, it was my way of coping. For me, anything was better than the gaping black hole that awaited me if I gave in." She takes a break to sniffle into a tissue. "You girls were too young to understand. I don't expect you to understand now, or ever."

"Jesus, Mom. I do understand." In moments of complete, blinding anger, I've resented my parents for having children in the first place, but I can hardly hold my own existence against them—despite trying to erase it.

"You and I, Ella," her voice croaks, "we're sensitive in a way your father and Nina will never fully comprehend."

"If you knew," I start to choke up, "what I inherited from you." It sounds so silly to say it like that. "Why didn't you reach out and offer help?"

"I did. So many times. You blew me off at the merest hint of intimacy between us. And I know that's on me and I'll carry that guilt with me forever." She looks away briefly. "I know what you think of me and it hurts me every single day."

I want to tell her it's not true. I'm squirming in my seat trying to come up with ways to deny that I've felt wronged by my own mother for more than half of my life, but nothing comes out. No more words make it past the knot in my throat.

We both stare at the lake, but, in that moment, its beauty is lost on me. The damage between my mother and me was done a long time ago. And perhaps knowledge is power, but, in this instant, it feels more like a heavy, crushing burden on my soul.

"What are you making for Kay tonight?" Mom breaks the silence.

"Roasted chicken with asparagus and bacon vinaigrette."

"Do you need a hand?"

I don't know what to say. Of all the surprising things my

mother has said since she arrived at the cabin, this suggestion amazes me the most. "Sure." I shuffle to the edge of my seat. "How about another glass of wine?"

"I would love that."

I know it's not much, but the light pang of relief running through me is, at least, something.

"It's my understanding she's quite fond of you," Mom says when I return with the bottle of wine.

I've been out to my parents for twenty years and I've never brought a girlfriend home, never even gave the possibility a second thought. I can't help but go on the defense. "I know you don't like her, but—"

"That's not what I'm trying to say, Ella. I couldn't be more thrilled for you if it worked out. I mean it."

"Yes, well, it's complicated."

For the time it takes us to finish that second glass of wine, my mother seems like a different person. Perhaps she feels temporarily freed from the crosses she bears in life. Or perhaps she's over the moon to have something that resembles a normal conversation with her daughter.

"I agree that love and relationships can be complicated, but, as your father would say, 'don't destroy it by overthinking it'." This strikes me as an exact phrase from Kay's big book of wisdom. It also shows me that the way I've thought about my parents' marriage all these years might have been a tad too superficial.

18

————

By the time Kay arrives I'm still so frazzled that her soft knock on the door startles me, but her presence, nonetheless, has an instant calming effects on my nerves—like that first dip in the lake after dark.

"I waited an hour after I saw your mother's car leave the lot. Not that I was counting down the minutes." She holds up a bottle of champagne.

"Are we celebrating something?" I lean my hip against the kitchen counter and look Kay over. She's wearing extra tight linen shorts and a halter top that accentuates her shoulders in a way that makes my mouth water.

"Our first date." She steps closer. "I was expecting smoke in your kitchen and the irresistible smell of burning meat. Color me surprised." While she hands me the bottle, she gazes deep into my eyes.

"My mom helped me cook." I fight the urge to lean into her, to feel her support.

"How are you?" Gently, she places a hand on my shoulder. "Are you in the mood for this?"

"I'm exhausted from slaving over this chicken." I point at the oven.

"How about I pour us a glass of that?" She nods at the bottle. "And we sit for a few minutes before we eat."

"Okay." The afternoon's tension slides off me with Kay's arrival, leaving my muscles limp, and my brain a numb mass.

I wait on the porch, in the same chair I sat in when my mother was here. After Kay has sat down and we've lifted our glasses, toasting what we insist on calling our 'first date', I glance at her, so relieved to sit opposite someone whose face relaxes me and whose presence doesn't undo me.

"She practically gave us her blessing." The bubbles burst on my tongue as I sip and scan Kay's face for a reaction.

"Well, that kind of takes all the fun out of it." A huge smile breaks on her face. "Seriously, though. Do you want to talk about it?"

I shake my head. I've done enough of that sort of talking for one day. "No. We made progress, I guess. Actually had a conversation. She shed some light on things that were never very clear to me, but now, I just want to be with you. Enjoy your company."

"Sounds good to me." The tenderness in Kay's smile all but floors me.

"I also really, really want to kiss you again." In the depths of my gut, I already know where this night is headed—how I *want* it to end.

"Now that we have your mother's blessing, I guess that can be arranged." Kay puts her glass on the table, leans back in her chair, pins her dark, sparkling eyes on me, and beckons me over with two fingers. "Come here."

My legs are grateful they only have to take two steps to reach Kay's chair. I plant my knees astride her thighs and sink down, peering at her from above.

Kay traces a finger across my cheekbone, down to my

lips, before clasping her hands behind my neck and pulling me close. When we kiss, everything falls away. It's just her and me. The lake behind us. The electricity between us. I haven't had a moment like this in years. A moment during which all thought stops, every thought process frozen, the merest inkling of a negative assumption killed instantly by the soft sensation of her lips, the gentle but distinct pull of her hands. The throbbing between my legs.

When we break for air and linger in the heavenly silence for a moment, the smell of burnt chicken reaches my nose.

"Oh, shit." I push myself off Kay and run to the kitchen.

"Careful," I hear her say from right behind me.

I grab the oven mitts from the counter and yank the tray out of the oven. The skin on top is charred to a black crisp, but most of it seems all right. Relieved, I turn off the oven and face her.

"Domestic goddess at your service." I burst out into a silly giggle. "The bird is ready."

"Don't worry, I like my chicken nice and crispy." Kay peers at the stove behind me. "Do you have anything else cooking?"

"No, the accompaniments are chilling in the fridge."

"Good." Kay nods and grabs my hand before pushing my back against the refrigerator. Her knee presses between my legs and her lips are hungry on mine. Looks like the chicken and I are not the only ones overheating.

I let my hands wander across her back, my fingers finding their way underneath the hem of her tank top, meeting skin. Kay's lips leave mine. She kisses my chin, starts on my neck, and I'm ready. I couldn't care less about the chicken, or the champagne, or Dr. Hakim, or all the faults in my personality. My mind is quiet, too saturated with lust and desire to start a debate on the appropriateness of this.

"Sorry." Kay pants, her eyes glazing over. "Lost control there for a minute."

Already, I miss her mouth on mine, her hands in my neck, her knee between my thighs. I shake my head, bite my lip. "I want you."

"God, I want you too." Her voice is a strangled whisper. "But let's eat first." She plants her palm on the door of the fridge next to my head. "You've gone to all this trouble." The back of her other hand caresses my jaw. "Besides, this frenzy is not exactly what I had in mind."

I understand what she means, but this frenzy is exactly what I need. Yet, I nod, yielding. In any event, it's probably not a bad idea to have a meal first.

"Are you all right?" Kay glares at me, the intensity in her eyes enough to make my knees buckle a bit. Since Thalia, I haven't been with anyone—not even with myself.

———

After Kay has pronounced my lemon-infused chicken a resounding, if surprising, success and we've loaded the plates into the dishwasher, I bring out the whiskey. I bought the brand Kay has made a habit of pouring me and the glint of approval in her glance probably satisfies me more than it should.

"You seem different tonight," she says, peering pensively over the lake. Night has all but fallen, the only remnant of the day a grayish sheen on the surface of the water, before it turns black again.

"Maybe I *am* different." I follow her gaze over the lake. "That's why I came here, after all." But I don't want to talk about myself anymore. I want to know about her.

"I've been meaning to ask." Kay turns toward me, beating me to asking her a question. "You keep saying that your romantic relationships tend to turn sour, that, after a while, you chase your girlfriends away… as a contender for that title"—a slight tilt of her lips—"I'm quite curious as to what exactly goes wrong."

I look deep into her eyes. *A contender for that title?* My skin breaks out in goose bumps. "I'll try to answer your question." My throat has gone dry. "But after that, you have to promise me it will be all about you."

Kay chuckles, but only briefly. "I solemnly swear to tell you a bedtime story about my youth." Her features fall into a serious expression. "I'm not asking to give you a hard time, Ella. I'm asking because I have no interest in being someone you fall for for all the wrong reasons." A new intensity glints in her eyes. "I'm not fooling around here."

I nod my understanding. Possibly, I've been too wrapped up in my own feelings to acknowledge that Kay has them, too. I inhale deeply—as if every breath I take at West Waters will clear my lungs of city debris—to win some time. "I guess, on the surface, despite being a science geek, I'm fairly easy to, uh, go for." I send her a shy smile. "And I have just enough game to lure someone into a first date, charm them and—if we like each other—set things in motion. When I fall in love, I tend to fall hard and fast." I have to clear my throat, because the case in point is too obvious. Saying the words out loud, it hits me that, ever since I arrived at West Waters, I've fallen into the same old trap—despite my trepidations and what I thought was careful monitoring of my emotions and motivations.

"Don't go there, Ella." Kay's voice startles me. *Can she read my mind?* "Just tell me what happened with Thalia."

I take a sip of whiskey, and another. *Thalia.* So out of my league I just had to have her, if only to prove to myself that, in the end, it could never work. Prove that kind of love was not for me.

"When I met Thalia, I basically lost my mind. Physically, she could not have resembled 'my type' more. Sometimes, despite how ugly it ended between us, when I think of Thalia, I still feel it. There was something about her smile that floored me. Something about the way she focused her attention on me when I talked that made me feel as if I were the world's most fascinating speaker. I met her and I had to give it a try. We met at her art exhibition and, somehow, we clicked. Something fell into place. Love at first sight and all of that. Within a month we were practically living together. All the lesbian stereotype boxes checked." I exhale a nervous giggle. "It was like the beginning of any new relationship. Intense. Delirious. I was careful to reveal my true self very slowly. Although I think I only started driving her totally crazy around the sixth month." I glance at Kay: eyes focused, sunk into pensive listener mode. Why am I telling her this? Will it make a difference?

"Thalia didn't have it all figured out either, but at least she didn't have my temper. I know I hide it well, but I have an extremely short fuse. When my brain crashes, just like a computer's hard drive can, everything goes black, and I lash out. I lose all perspective because, in my mind, it's all turning to shit so fast, I can't keep up. Much like a spoiled toddler who doesn't get her way. No more big picture. Just vile, ugly words pouring from my mouth."

It's the built-up anger inside of you trying to find a way out, Dr. Hakim said the first time I tried to tell him about that.

"I don't know if it's because snide remarks, unfair criticism, and sudden outbursts of anger were *de rigueur* when I was growing up, or if it's just another fabulous personality trait I inherited from my mother… Perhaps a bit of both." I can't look at Kay anymore. "But I do know it's the root of most of my problems. A poisonous temper will destroy the best of relationships, and it doesn't exactly help with my self-image either. Always having to pick up the pieces, apologizing for things I said in the heat of the moment, facing myself in the mirror after another senseless fit of rage. Because, in the end, it's hardly ever about the other person. It only happens because, most days, I hate myself so much." The tears come again. "A bit of a self-fulfilling prophecy, actually." I find a stray napkin on the table and dab it against my eyes.

"I never told anyone about this, only my doctor." In that respect, Kay could not be more different from Thalia. "I've been working on it with him. Learning to recognize the signs, to start with. Trying to eliminate the origin of the rage and feelings of hatred. Reprogram my behavior, basically."

"The real reason why you came back." Kay's voice sounds more hesitant than I've ever heard it. Not even someone with her patience and inherent wisdom can easily process what I just said. She's also not my therapist. A few hours ago we were making out like frisky teenagers, now, every notion of romance has fled.

I nod, certain I have blown my chances with her as well. I said too much. Revealed too much of my darkness. This is not chatter for a first date. "You don't have to stay," I whisper. "I understand."

"What kind of friend would that make me?"

Friend? A mere half hour ago she referred to herself as a potential girlfriend.

"Maybe it's best if you go, either way." Somehow, I manage to squeeze the words out of my throat, despite a big red warning sign flashing in my brain. This is why Dr. Hakim and I both agreed I shouldn't get involved with someone at this time. It was always going to be too messy, too confusing, too destructive—and too distracting.

"Ella?" There's hurt in Kay's voice now. "Don't do this. Break the pattern. Recognize the signs." I hear a sniffling sound coming from Kay's end of the table, but I still can't look at her.

"Why would you want me, Kay? There's nothing here." Frustrated, I tap my chest. "Only gloom and loss and disappointment."

"Do you really think I'm going to let you do this after what you've just told me?"

"Fine." I glare at her from under my lashes, taken aback by the sheen of tears on her cheeks, but, obviously, not taken aback enough. "Be my *friend*. I suppose life can get quite boring here at West Waters. How about I'll be *your* distraction this Indian summer?"

"You can hold yourself in as low a regard as you damn well wish, Ella. Drown in your sea of negativity all you want. But I know why you came here and it wasn't to insult me." She shakes her head. "I refuse to be insulted by you, by what is clearly a result of your vulnerability."

The force with which she delivers her argument takes the steam out of my trip into familiar dark, all-obliterating territory. I bite back the next venomous words that sit at the ready at the tip of my tongue.

"I also refuse to believe you only have bad sides. Would I be sitting here if I didn't see the beauty in you? The kindness you're so desperate to hide? The only thing that stands between this version of yourself you created in your head and the real, accomplished, smart, sensible, gorgeous woman that you are, is you, Ella. I won't pretend to know what goes on in that tortured mind of yours, and I won't sit here and proclaim it's easy, but the truth is that it's only as hard as you make it on yourself. And you're making it very hard on yourself."

"I can't even roast a chicken properly." I don't mean it as a joke. In the state I'm in, everything is deadly serious, even something as silly and unimportant as the chicken.

"Only because I distracted you." To my relief, Kay doesn't laugh. Instead, she continues, "I guess the greatest thing you can achieve in life is to be completely at ease with yourself. To accept yourself for who you are, faults and all. I also believe that very few people ever reach that level of supreme enlightenment. The thing is, you don't have to be perfect. It's not a requirement for happiness."

"You seem to be doing a pretty great job."

Kay gives a loud huff. "What? Because I hang around here all day hoping to catch a glimpse of you?" She shoots me a crooked smile. "That's only because I'm smitten."

The warm glow from earlier descends on me again. I refrain from making a self-deprecating comment. Instead, I scan Kay's face. Her almond-shaped eyes. Her nut-brown skin. Her lips. As much as I want to kiss them again, I'm too exhausted to even make it out of my chair, my body a limp mass of flesh and bones.

"This was not how it was supposed to go."

"Or maybe it was." Kay pours us both a bit more whiskey. "Either way, we have all the time in the world."

19

I wake up with Kay's arm around me. My brain is fuzzy from the crying and the whiskey, but alert enough to remember that nothing happened, only a replay from the night before. I check the alarm clock. It's 4.30 in the morning and, outside, the first light hasn't broken through yet. Kay purrs softly behind me, her breath hot on the skin of my neck. Deep inside me, the throbbing ignites. It doesn't help that her breasts poke against my back and that, when I glance down, I catch a glimpse of her strong, long fingers.

Slowly, I try to slide onto my back, attempting not to disturb her too much, but once I've managed to roll over, her hand rests dangerously close to my breast. Despite wearing a t-shirt, my nipple instantly reaches upward and any chance of more sleep leaves the room.

Kay stirs in her sleep, her breath on my cheek now, her chin resting on my shoulder. Physically, we could be closer, I guess, but not by much. It's in my heart I feel closest to her, anyway. She stayed. She listened to me and decided not to leave.

In the circles I moved in in Boston—brainy university

couples, glitzy art crowds, gay men in designer clothes and no one boasting less than a master's degree—I never came across someone like Kay, and if I had, I most likely wouldn't have given her the time of day. I always went for the likes of Thalia, well-dressed, well-off and no qualms about showing it. Mouthy, well-spoken women who wouldn't dream of jumping into a lake naked. Women who had their heads too far up their own asses to give a much needed conversation an extra five minutes, or who reacted to one of my outbursts with stone-cold silence—the kind I knew so well from being raised by my mother.

Of course, it wasn't Thalia's fault that I could never live up to what the combination of my dreamy blue eyes, high cheekbones and job title promised. Thalia's words, not mine.

With Thalia, the *coup de foudre* was purely physical. Hormones racing through my blood, clouding my judgment. Of all the antidepressants I ever ingested, not one ever beat the rush of falling in love.

It takes almost more willpower than I have to not trace a finger over Kay's hand, to not cup her hand with my palm and press it against my breast. But with her, it's different. The entire approach is opposite to what I'm used to. Falling in love and busting it up. Curing heartbreak by going out into the night in search of a fresh dopamine shot, when I'd much rather stay in to read a book. The endless cycle of work, chase, thrill, something-close-enough-to-love-to-tide-me-over, break-up, more work. As long as I didn't have to stop to think about what I was doing with my life —and why.

But every cycle broke me a little more until, after Thalia, I looked in the mirror and knew I couldn't go out there anymore. Not because I was certain I had lost the love of my life—as I had been so many times before—but because it was obvious that I hadn't. So what was I crying for?

"Penny for your thoughts." Kay's fingers dig into the flesh just under my breast.

"Hey." She could give a million dollars for my thoughts, it would be in vain because my brain stopped working the instant her fingers pressed down. "Didn't mean to wake you." I try to keep my body as still as possible.

"What time is it?"

"Around five, I think." Kay's hand balls into a fist, grabbing onto the fabric of my t-shirt. The first soft light of dawn makes its way underneath the curtains.

"Sleep like a log again?" Her voice is still warm with sleepiness.

"Not this time." I clear my throat. "I think that, this time around, I was the one who couldn't keep certain images out of my head."

Kay's early morning chuckle is much sweeter than her middle-of-the-day belly roar. "Is that so?" She relaxes her fingers and fans them out, the tip of her thumb touching the underside of my breast. "Can you describe the images to me? Maybe I can help." Despite the early hour, an urgency has already started creeping into her voice.

I shake my head, my cheek bumping into her nose. "But I *can* show you." At last, I grab her hand, hold her fingers hard against my skin.

Kay doesn't need much encouragement and, just like I thought she always would, she takes control. Her hand, still covered with mine, sneaks upward and cups my breast. Through the fabric of my t-shirt, my nipple pokes hard against her palm, straining, wanting more.

Kay pushes herself up on her other arm and looks down at me. No words are needed. I suspect my eyes are blazing with desire, screaming that I'm ready, that I want her. Now.

While her fingers massage my breast—nothing tentative about the motion anymore—Kay leans down and kisses me.

Our mouths are closed at first, but only for a few seconds. Soon, her tongue darts between my lips and the kiss deepens while two of Kay's fingers close around my nipple. My body stiffens at her pinch, and our lips lose touch. When I open my eyes and look into Kay's face, I see nothing but lust and understanding and, perhaps, acceptance. Kay sees me with different eyes, through a lens that, maybe, no one has ever seen me through before and, most astonishingly, she's still here. And although I didn't come back to Northville for this, in this moment, it feels like everything I've ever wanted, for all the right reasons, is compressed into that glance.

It's as if something has gone off in Kay's brain. Still controlled, but with much more purpose, her hand slides down my t-shirt and, in a flash, underneath. Her fingers on my skin produce an entirely different sensation, leaving me panting into her mouth as her lips crash down onto mine again.

While this is also about release, about undoing the tension that's been building between us for days, the main qualifier is intimacy. Because that too has been growing. As mindless as that first moment of surrender may be, that instant I give myself up to her, offer myself into her beautiful, strong hands, I'm there all the way. All of me shows up when Kay's fingers close around my nipple without any barriers for the first time. My heart and my soul are in the next kiss we share.

My t-shirt has ridden up, but only exposes my belly. I want to feel more of her. Awkwardly, I start hoisting up her t-shirt, but half of her body is in the way.

"Hold on." Kay pushes herself away from me for an instant and yanks her t-shirt over her head. Although I've seen her naked before—in a hurry in the dark—this time could not be more different. My eyes are glued to her breasts, the darkness of her tiny nipples, the sheen of her skin in the brightening morning light. I push myself up so I can lay my hands on her chest. Kay kneels next to me and I mirror her image, only briefly refraining from touching her so she can remove my t-shirt. We sit opposite each other, naked from the waist up, and the fire that rages in my stomach is nothing compared to the wild thumping between my legs.

I guess, for the sake of romance, and perhaps memory, this should go slowly: deliberate movements stealing over our skin, finding the right spots. Not this frenzy, as Kay said last night. But my fingers itch with the desire for frantic groping and my body is ready for abandon, for mindlessness, for giving myself up to her completely in a tangle of flesh, skin, hair, and limbs.

I dreamed of Kay entering me slowly while she gazed into my eyes, but it's not how I want her now. It's as though I step out of myself, out of this body and, especially, this mind that has constrained me for so long. I lunge for her. Like a tiger, I throw myself on top of her. Our breasts collide and Kay topples over onto her back. I'm not too far gone to check if this is what she wants, but when our eyes meet, there's no room for doubt. This is not the same Kay who came for me last night, who pressed me against the door of the fridge with all her might, only to pull back when the kiss got too intense.

She's been seeing the same images in her mind, I can tell.

"I want to feel you," I hiss, my hand traveling down toward her panties, but she beats me to it, yanking down her knickers while my body breathes heavily on top of her.

I give her space to take off her underpants and get rid of my own in the process. Looking at her, completely naked in my bed, gives me pause. Because as much as it is frenzy and lust and two bodies bursting with desire, it's so much more than that. It's love. Or, at least, the beginning of it. It's more than falling in love, more than hormones going bonkers in my blood, more than the crazy pull of chemistry bringing us together. Because, despite only just really getting to know each other, Kay already knows me better than anyone. It intensifies the rapid beat of blood in my veins, the quick pulse of my heart vibrating throughout my body, the electricity on my skin.

For all the times I believed I was making love, to Thalia and every other woman that came before her, I know now that I was wrong. Any lingering trace of doubt in my mind about giving in to this, about being with Kay interfering with my healing process, evaporates at the sight of her beneath me. Because it's not just her body in front of me, waiting with bated breath, it's all of her and all of me, about to be joined together. For the first time since I woke up in the hospital, I actually feel, all the way into my bones, that I'm happy to be alive.

Tears sting behind my eyes, but I ignore them, because, for once, they're the right kind of tears. I lift myself off her and extend my hand to Kay. She grabs it, pulling herself up. We sit on our knees facing each other again, a calmness clinging to the anticipation of what is about to transpire. I slide my knees apart and pull her toward me. From the movement of the sheets below me, I deduct she's doing the same. Both of us kneeling, open, ready, spread wide for each other.

My breath picks up speed when we kiss again, when our rock hard nipples bounce off each other, my arms pulling her as close as I can. My right hand wanders down, as does hers, meeting in the small space we left between our bellies. Our mouths stay connected, like our souls now, while our hands drift apart: mine between her legs, hers between mine.

The double sensation of feeling Kay there for the first time and her touching me where I haven't been touched in a long time, nearly floors me. I have to hold on to her for

148

support, lifting my body a little higher, my one elbow resting on her shoulder.

Her breath in my mouth, her flesh so close to mine I can feel the rhythm of her heart against my skin, her finger hovering over my pussy lips. And then, stars colliding in my brain, a wave of pleasure rolling over me, as her finger circles my clit. Slowly at first, small, controlled circles through the wetness that has pooled there. And I do the same to her, only my finger slides along the length of her pussy. My breath catches in my throat at how wet she is for me. How ready.

How many days ago did I arrive at West Waters? Is that when the foreplay started? It doesn't matter, because Kay's finger becomes more insistent, and I try to follow her pace. I dip lower, brace my core, and let my finger slide inside of her. It cuts off my own breath because her arm pulls me closer, losing control of her hand in my hair, the fingers of her other hand zoning in on my swollen clit again.

It's difficult to not give in to the pangs of pleasure tumbling down my stomach, the lightning in my blood, but I'm on a mission as well. My finger burrows deep inside of Kay. Our kiss has stalled. My mouth hangs open in front of Kay's face, ragged puffs of breath pulsing out of me to the rhythm of my thrusts. I add another finger, trying to ignore how my own pleasure mounts, how my entire body thunders toward climax—but it's been so long and this is too much. All this blood flowing freely in my veins. My heart beating so exuberantly, after I wanted to make it stop.

Kay's finger is insistent, rubbing tiny circles around my clit, faster, creating a vibrating sensation, and I give up, because the orgasm takes me—months of release gushing out from between my legs, all the muscles in my body shaking, my mouth open wide, my eyes filled with tears. Involuntarily, my finger slips out of her as I collapse on top of her.

She cradles me in her arms while I catch my breath. *I*

didn't used to be like this, I think. I used to require a whole lot more than a finger rubbing along my clit to make me come, but I realize it's not about what she did to me with her hands. It's about how she made me feel. Alive. Safe. Understood.

I revive quickly with Kay's arms around me and when I straighten my posture, I see she's crying as well. Just a few tiny drops caught in the corner of her eyes, but tears nonetheless.

"Are you all right?" I ask, instinctively.

"Oh yes." A grin breaks through the grave expression on her face. "I barely touched you. Was it one of those spiritual orgasms?"

I want to wave away her silly comment, but it hits me that it may just have been. Biology is my profession. I have extensive knowledge of the human body's blood flow, its nerve endings, and the chemical and biological processes related to orgasm. Still, in my heart, I acknowledge there was more to this particular climax than the cause and effect of fingers on my clit in a highly aroused state. But I have neither time nor inclination to ponder this further. I have unfinished business.

"I guess my clit is rather fond of your fingers." I chuckle at the silliness of my own comment.

"And my fingers want to touch a whole lot more of you." Kay grins.

I tip my head and rest my eyes on her. "That may very well be, but they're going to have to wait." I put my hands on her shoulders and start lowering her onto the bed. I gaze down at her, into her sparkling, dark eyes, and I feel saved already. More of a functioning person than when I woke up earlier this morning.

I drape my body half onto hers, leaving enough room to let my fingers wander over her skin.

"Don't tease me, Ella." Kay's voice is firm. "I need it now."

Time to finish what I started. The exact opposite of what I fantasized about happens. Instead of Kay slowly bringing her fingers to my wet pussy lips, I'm the one slipping the tip of my finger along her folds while looking deep into her eyes. I hold my hand still for an instant, locking my gaze on hers again, and go deep with two fingers. Her muscles stiffen underneath me, her eyes falling shut. Her moan is the most beautiful sound in the world. It's still a little bit controlled, but frayed enough around the edges to distinguish it from any other sound in any other circumstance. It's the sound of promise, of things to come.

I move slowly inside of her, feeling the velvety inside of her pussy. The hotness seems to shoot straight through my fingers, making my clit throb again.

I give my fingers more purpose, more thrusting than feeling, fucking her—fucking Kay Brody. Underneath me, the sight is magical. Kay's head tossed back into the pillows, her breasts moving to the rhythm of my strokes, her skin glistening in the morning light, her pelvis bucking upward. The sight of ecstasy. To think I would have missed this had my attempt not failed.

While upping my pace and starting to brush my thumb over her clit at slow intervals, I close my lips around her nipple. I'm as close to her as I can be. Inside of her, on top of her, my lips on her—her body surrendering to me. I inhale the scent of her skin, of that body that has been glued to mine for two nights in a row.

"Oh god," Kay moans, her breath stuttering in between the sounds she utters. She's close, I can feel it in the contractions of her muscles, the tautness of her skin, so I clamp down on her nipple harder, increase the depth of my strokes and let my thumb hover over her clit, allowing her to choose the amount of pressure applied.

Kay's nails delve deep into my flesh, possibly breaking skin—a mark I'll proudly carry—while the back of her head disappears further into the pillow, exposing her neck. Then her body relaxes, her limbs falling to her side. Her eyes are still closed as I kiss her neck, her chin, her slightly parted lips.

"I won't be able to speak for a few minutes," Kay huffs. She opens her arms wide and I nestle against her shoulder, listening to the wild pitter-patter of her heart. We lie in complete, blissful silence for a while.

Out of nowhere, a loud banging on the cabin door startles us.

"What the—" Kay's body goes rigid, toppling me off her.

I check the alarm clock. It's not even six in the morning. Did I switch my phone off? Did something happen to Mom or Dad? In a panic, I scramble for clothes, quickly throwing on the t-shirt I slept in and hoping it's long enough to cover me while I answer the door.

"Maybe it's for me," Kay hollers behind me.

I unlock the front door, peeking my head through the crack, trying to hide most of my body. I have to blink twice before I recognize the person standing in front of me, before it registers.

"Hope I didn't wake you, Sis," Nina says, an undecipherable smile on her face.

20

"K ay? Is that you?" Nina's accent sounds different. She looks healthy, lean but in a wiry, sinewy way. Her skin has tanned to a deep cinnamon color. Her bleached hair is pulled back in a messy ponytail. For someone who, most likely, just got off a flight from the other end of the world, she looks surprisingly well put together.

Behind me, Kay grumbles something. I'm still too flabbergasted to move, and painfully aware of not wearing any underwear.

"Were you two…?" Nina's face breaks out into a wide, knowing smile. "What the hell, Ellie? I know we're not the kind, but give your big sister a hug, will you?" She steps forward, arms wide.

I make my way from behind the door, pulling the t-shirt down as best I can, but it barely covers my behind. It doesn't matter though, because when Nina wraps her arms around me and holds me close—when it sinks in that my sister whom I haven't seen in the flesh for years, is here—I relax and let the tears come.

"What are you doing here?" I ask, while wetting her top with my tears.

"Do you have to ask? What on earth have you done, Ellie? I was so worried about you."

Any other person would have sent an e-mail to announce her arrival, but not my sister. Being like everyone else was never high on Nina Goodman's wish list. "I wasn't expecting you to come here."

We break from our hug. Nina eyes my skimpy attire. "Well, I'm here anyway. Why don't you put some clothes on to celebrate?"

While I rush to the bedroom to find a pair of shorts, the smell of sex penetrating my nostrils, I hear muffled voices from the living room.

"Last I heard you were shacked up with Jeff Mitchum." I hear Nina say when I re-enter the living room.

"That was a long time ago, Nina." Kay is not easily fazed, though, and Nina's sudden arrival doesn't throw her as much as it does me.

"Swinging both ways, huh? Good for you." Nina practically thumps Kay in the biceps. I can tell she hasn't changed much. Apart from the blood flowing in our veins, we never had that much in common.

"I'd best leave you girls to it." Kay finds my eyes and I give her a nod. When she heads to the bedroom I follow her in there briefly.

"I can't believe it."

"That's Nina Goodman for you." Kay scans the room for the clothes she was wearing yesterday. "Go be with your sister, Ella."

I step closer to her and fold my arms around her waist. "Sorry about the interruption."

"Don't worry about that. I'll be around later." She plants

a chaste kiss on the top of my head and frees herself from my embrace.

I shoot her one last longing glance before rejoining my sister in the living room. Kay stumbles out not long after me.

"See you later, Goodmans," she says, before closing the front door behind her.

"Coffee?" I eye Nina. The shock is starting to subside.

Nina nods. "Fuck, Ellie. Why did you do it?" Nina is always best at asking the questions everyone else is trying to avoid. Yet another reason why she couldn't stay.

"You can't just turn up here out of the blue and ask me that." I lean against the kitchen counter, not making any moves toward brewing coffee.

"I came all this way. Sixteen hours folded into an economy class seat. Excuse me if I can't find my manners and tact. It must be jet lag."

"Nina." I use the same tone I used to scold her with as a child—and I was the younger sister.

"Damn, Ellie. I don't know what to say." She shakes her head. "But I sure am bloody glad to see you." Did she always swear like that?

"Do you want to take a shower? Freshen up?" I offer.

"You and Brody, huh? How long's that been going on?"

As happy as I am to see my sister, somehow, it's so incredibly like her to pick a time like this to arrive, and ruin a very special moment. "Not long."

"First time?" She arches up her eyebrows suggestively.

"Yes." I inch closer toward her. "You know where the bathroom is. Get cleaned up. I'll have breakfast ready when you're done. Then we can talk."

"Still bossing your big sister around, Ellie? You haven't changed."

"Neither have you." I watch her saunter off to the bathroom, waiting until she's closed the door behind her to collapse in a chair.

The memory of Kay's hands on me is still so fresh in my mind, it's hard to focus on the fact that Nina just walked into the cabin. For someone who used to pride herself on bouts of ultra-efficient multi-tasking, my mind goes into melt-down mode too easily. Perhaps also because Nina definitely has the Goodman stubbornness, but as far as non-conversations go—especially the kind my mother, father, and I excel at—Nina is not like the rest of us. And spending years away, doing god-knows-what who-knows-where, hasn't sharpened her sense of tact, so it seems. She will ask the hard questions, and she won't wait for an answer.

I get up to wash my hands before making toast and laying out some condiments on the table on the deck. I wish Kay were still here, but I also know that, once again, this is something I have to face alone.

When Nina reemerges, smelling of soap and wearing a fresh set of clothes, out of the blue, she hugs me again. Perhaps she *has* changed. It's hard to take stock when most of my memories of her were made before I left Northville myself.

"I'm so sorry, Ellie." Her eyes are moist when she lets go of me and scans my face. "For leaving you behind. With them."

"I'll be right back." I hurry into the bathroom to rinse my face. I steady myself against the sink and take a long hard look at myself in the mirror. My mother's visit yesterday afternoon, my emotional date with Kay, what happened this morning, and now Nina. When Dr. Hakim told me about potential emotionally stressful moments—and how to cope with them—I doubt he had this in mind. *You have the luxury of time, Ella,* he said. *Spread the load.*

I take a deep breath and look into my own eyes. They're the same as Nina's—a bright blue inheritance from our dad.

When I arrive back on the deck, I find two whiskey glasses with a finger of liquid in them on the table next to the breakfast food.

"It's the middle of the night for me," Nina says. "I need a pick-me-up."

"You must be exhausted." Grateful for the booze, albeit on an empty stomach, I sink into a chair next to her.

"It's all relative, I guess." She holds up her glass. "Here's to you, Little Sister. And to the exciting family reunion in our very near future."

The alcohol practically burns my throat as it goes down, but I welcome its numbing effects.

"Mom and Dad will be over the moon."

"We'll see about that." Nina puts her glass down and picks up a piece of toast. "I know it's a bit cramped, but can I stay here with you? I really can't face staying at the house."

"Of course."

"I take it you'll be spending your nights at Kay's, anyway." She winks at me the way Kay sometimes does. "She was always the serious type, even in high school. Like you, Ellie." Nina slants her head. "How do you feel about the whole bisexual thing, though? I mean, I'll be honest with you, I've dabbled, but it's just not for me, you know?" Nina's babbling. She must be wrecked with nerves about this whole situation as well. She probably booked her ticket on impulse, before she gave herself the chance to really think about why she was coming back in the first place.

"It's early days." As much as I'd like to spend the day talking about Kay, it feels unsavory. I don't want what I have with Kay to be the subject of nervous chatter like this. "We'll see. But I'm extremely fond of her." A tiny bolt of lightning runs through me as I say the words.

"I can tell," Nina says between munching toast, but how could she possibly be able to tell? She hasn't seen me for years.

"How about you? Anyone special in your life?" The mere fact that I have to ask my own sister this question is reason enough to have another sip of whiskey.

"My men come and go." Nina shrugs. "I've never been particularly good with commitment. I wonder why." She gazes out over the lake. "This place does have charm." She seems keen to change the subject. "But you should come visit me in New Zealand, Sis. Nature like you wouldn't believe. Much too stunning to try to put into words."

Maybe you should send us some pictures from time to time, I think, but refuse to say out loud out of fear of sounding too much like Mom. It hits me that, since Nina arrived, I've been able to identify with almost every emotion—no matter how bitter —my mother has ever expressed about her oldest daughter's departure. It's moments like these that are the hardest to bear. The moments in which I realize that it wasn't coming back to Northville that required a certain amount of courage, it's all the conversations I've yet to have. The road to some form of forgiveness I need to find somewhere in my heart. No matter how far my sister and I both run, we can't outrun the simple fact that we share DNA with the people who made and raised us. We are versions of them, with our own beliefs and unique traits, very different but, also, in many ways, the same. We've both tried, but we can't outrun who we are.

"Perhaps I will." I pin my eyes on my sister's face. The fatigue is starting to break through. The vivid complexion of her skin is beginning to fade, as is that sparkle in her eye. "How do you keep busy up there?"

"You mean *down* there?" I sense sadness in Nina's tone, but she shakes it off well. She inhales deeply before speaking again. "When I left Northville, I made one single promise to myself: to never become like *them*." She doesn't need to qualify who 'them' are. "I think I succeeded pretty well. I never bought into the marriage-with-two-point-four-kids myth. I'm so glad you haven't either, Ellie. I knew from a young age that I didn't want to impart my genes on an innocent baby. That I would never want a child of mine to feel the way I felt when I was growing up." The way she says it makes it sound like a rehearsed speech. "And I know it's tragic, this anger I still carry inside of me, like I never grew out of that parent-hating phase of adolescence. I've given up a lot for it, but never for one second have I felt as if I had any other choice."

It's as though Nina has reached into my brain, scooped out the words, and laid them on her own tongue. Still, in this moment of sudden sisterly camaraderie and understanding, because of what my mother told me yesterday afternoon, I feel the need to defend our parents.

"Do you know about Mom's, uh, condition?"

An awkward chuckle makes its way out of Nina's throat. Shaking her head, she brings the glass she's been cradling in her hands to her mouth and takes a sip. "I do." She drinks again, emptying her glass. "But possibly only because Dad, in a desperate attempt to make me like him again after his sordid little affair came out, told me everything. How he'd been *forced* to take care of me while Mom was *away*. And how unusual that was for a man back then in the seventies. The last scrap of respect I still had for him went out of the window that day." She blows some air through her nostrils. "He truly believed the things he said could make me change my mind about him." With a bang, she deposits the glass on the table. "Oh the sacrifices he made by staying with Mom. He could have left her so easily, but he stayed, because she needed him. He was one of the good guys, did I not see that?

The thing is, Ellie, that when someone needs to ask you to see the good in them, it hasn't exactly been showing in the first place."

I might be the professor, but it seems to me that Nina is much better at explaining difficult processes. I also realize that, perhaps, having her around could have made a big difference in my own life.

"And then," Nina isn't finished yet, "when he had the chance to actually show me how much he cared, he fucked it all up." Nina inhales sharply. She sneaks her hand over the table toward mine. "Except for leaving you behind, Ellie, I have no regrets. None."

Hesitantly, I place my palm on her hand.

"For all I care, they don't even need to know I'm here. I only came for you." Nina's eyes are watery when she looks at me, which leads me to believe she doesn't mean what she's saying. She's come to heal as well.

21

After Nina has succumbed to fatigue completely—aided by another glass of whiskey—I shower and make my way to the shop. I find Kay sorting through a delivery of breakfast bars and, instantly, my stomach starts rumbling. My insides tied in too many knots by Nina's sudden appearance, I didn't touch any of the food I laid out for breakfast. Now that I catch a glimpse of Kay, with her back to me, her behind already looking so familiar in a pair of shorts, the storm inside me settles somewhat, but only to make room for a different kind of restlessness in my blood. Kay. An hour of reminiscing with my sister hasn't tempered my desire for Kay. All I want is to pick up where we left things before that knock on the door earlier this morning. And even more than that, I want her inside of me.

"Excellent way to lure in customers." I lean against the counter and enjoy how my voice startles Kay.

A bunch of breakfast bars still in her hand, Kay turns toward me, an eager smile on her lips. "Here." She tosses me one. "I seem to have ordered too many."

I catch the protein bar with a reflexive movement of my

hand. As much as I want to tear off the wrapper and put it in my mouth, I'd much rather peel away Kay's clothes and press my lips to her skin. But she keeps on standing there, about two feet away, and something inside of me—the same old nagging feeling of doubt—keeps me from walking up to her.

"How's your sister?" Kay cocks up an eyebrow.

"Out for the count." Desire courses through me at the sight of Kay sinking her teeth into her bottom lip. "Long journey and she's no spring chicken anymore."

"Right." Kay nods, her bottom lip half sucked into her mouth. "Just like me, you mean?"

"I don't remember saying that." It doesn't matter what we say to each other, though. Just being near her is enough. Even standing a few feet away, I can feel the heat radiating off her body—I can feel that she hasn't had enough of me, either. "You don't still have a crush on her, do you?"

"Not sure, but either way, I guess I can make do with the little sister." Kay drops the bars back into the box by her feet and takes a step in my direction. She might as well have pinched my nipple between her fingers, that's how her close-ness affects me. And I know, more than I've ever known anything in my life, that before I can face any more of my family members—before I take Nina home—I need Kay. I need her arms around me, her lips on my skin, her fingers between my legs.

Unable to hold back any longer, no matter the endless string of doubts in my mind, my legs lead me to her. One step is all it takes. I smell her soap, her familiar scent, before she wraps her arms around me and finds my ear with her lips. "Are you okay?" she asks. "Not too shaken by Nina's sudden return?" But I don't want to talk about Nina any more. I want to go back to that blissful state I was in moments before she arrived. Not to undo her arrival, but because for as long as I can possibly remember, I haven't felt so safe with someone as I do with Kay. So understood. So accepted. So incredibly aroused.

"Take me inside," I manage to whisper. "To your bedroom."

"And close the shop at this hour of the day?" Although I can't see Kay's face, I hear the smile in her voice.

"Yes." I nod, my chin bumping against her shoulder. "Please."

"Anything for Nina Goodman's sister." She plants a kiss just below my ear, a kiss that is soft and hard at the same time. Soft and delicate with tenderness, but hard and clear in its intention.

Kay grabs my hand, shuts the door of the shop and displays the 'Closed' sign in the window. By the time we've reached the lodge, we're both practically running. We head straight for Kay's sparsely decorated bedroom, stopping only to catch our breath, before lunging for each other, hands frantic, skin on fire.

"Fuck me," I breathe into Kay's mouth when we kiss. "Please, fuck me." It makes her pull back from our kiss.

"Is that what you want?" Her voice is all gravel.

"It's all I want."

A smirk slips along her lips. "I will." Her eyebrows arch up when she says it, forcing a shudder of red hot lust up my spine. "But let's slow you down first." With that, her lips are back on my neck, planting gentle pecks, kissing their way up, along my throat, to my chin, until they reach my mouth. With her lips parted, she hovers over my mouth for a long second, before allowing her tongue to slither out, finding mine, her lips now firmly planted on mine.

I tug at her t-shirt, hoisting it off her, my fingers on her skin, their tips sizzling with the connection of flesh on flesh. Her tongue is already claiming me and my pelvis involuntarily crashes into hers. Kay lends a hand, breaking our kiss, her eyes not leaving mine, to get rid of her t-shirt and toss it, rather theatrically, behind her on the floor. I take the occasion to disrobe of as many items of my own clothing as I can, yanking my t-shirt over my head, my hands already searching for the clasp of my bra.

"Easy." Kay presses her full weight against me. "Let me do that." She covers my hands with hers and, together, we unhook my bra. Slowly, with one finger, she brushes a strap off my shoulder, then the other. Her eyes are glued to my chest as my bra slides away, exposing my breasts to the air, which always feels different with her. More charged. More infused with the possibility of happiness.

Unexpectedly, Kay grabs my wrists with both hands and pins them above my head. She curls the fingers of one hand around both my wrists, while bringing her other hand behind her back. I could easily force my hands down, but it's the last thing I want to do. I watch Kay unclasp her own bra with one hand. It doesn't get treated with the same reverence as mine and it comes off quickly, revealing her dark, taut nipples. She lets go of my wrists for a fraction of a second to toss her bra to the floor. There's that ripple of lust again, as her palm reconnects with my wrists, riding swiftly through my blood, making my heart beat faster.

Another new sensation: I can literally feel myself getting wet. Simply by looking at Kay, at the quick rise and fall of her breasts and the desire she expresses, I can feel my panties getting soaked in my own juices.

"I'll fuck you." Kay's voice has transformed into a low growl. Her left hand keeps my wrists above my head, and the power in it arouses me as much as it surprises me. Her other hand approaches my cheek, and its gentleness stands in stark contrast to the pure want sizzling in my flesh—the immediacy of it, the wanting it here-and-now quality of my own desire. I can also clearly see that same desire in every move she makes. She traces a finger to my lips, lets it hover before pressing down, not hard, but unmistakable in its intention.

Without saying a word, Kay pushes two fingers into my mouth and I suck on them for dear life. I want to pull her into my mouth as deep as I want her fingers in my pussy later. My tongue twirls around them, eager to show her what I can do—what I will do—with it. It's a way for me to make my intentions clear as well. My teeth bite gently on her fingers as she starts to retract them, her eyes still on me, peering equally as deep into my soul.

And if this is not saving me, then I don't know what could. Not in the way Dr. Hakim warned me about, but in this beautiful, lust-riddled, loving, healing way Kay has with me. Perhaps I have no way of knowing. Maybe my brain suffered damage while I was unconscious in the hospital. Knowing isn't even the right verb, because it can't possibly capture the sensation that flows through me. This feeling—or knowledge—that with her, with Kay, I'm approaching a version of myself I actually want to be. Because, simply by being herself, she lets me be myself.

With a dirty sucking sound, Kay's fingers leave my lips. She has me guessing and—aside from having been told in no uncertain terms that she *will* fuck me—I have no way of anticipating her next move. So, it is with awe, and another bout of lust tumbling down my stomach, that I watch her bring her fingers to her own lips, smearing my saliva on them, before sucking them into her mouth.

My hands are still above my head, my breasts protruding, my nipples so hard they almost hurt. I scan Kay's face as she licks her own fingers, coats them in more wetness. My clit throbs beneath my clothes. Instinctively, I know I shouldn't speak, so I tilt my head a little instead, try to express my need for those fingers inside of me with my eyes.

HARPER BLISS

Just like that, she frees my wrists from her grasp and they fall limply to my sides. Apparently, Kay needs both hands to rip my shorts off me. She crouches, fisting the fabric in her palms, her face so close to my pussy, I feel another spontaneous wave of wetness letting loose between my legs. The instant she tosses my shorts away, I spread wide, my knees already buckling, every cell in my body ready for her.

When her face is level with mine again, most of the everpresent kindness in Kay's eyes has been drummed away by glimmers of fierce lust, of a desire so great that if anyone came knocking on the door now, no matter who, we would ignore it. Because there's only us in the world in this moment. Only Kay Brody and Ella Goodman. I want to go back to that clearing in the woods and carve our names in a tree, etch the letters so deep into the trunk not even time can erase them.

The universe has narrowed to Kay and me. I'm standing with my legs spread, nothing but wild lust running through my veins, gazing into the storm raging in Kay's eyes. In the depths of my depression, when the darkness had taken so much from me that I was willing to give my life, if I could ever have had the strength to envision a moment to live for, it would have been this one. And, perhaps subconsciously, hidden deep beneath the pain and the despair that encased me, that moment already existed. Because I lived and here I am.

I'm naked and ready, my blood a stream of hot, pulsing lava, pooling in my clit. I curve my arms around Kay's waist, drag her closer, our bare breasts colliding, but she pushes away from me. Her gaze is intense, as though sliding her fingers inside me is some sort of reverent moment and, maybe it is, but the need that keeps on growing inside my belly does not agree. Yet, I still don't say the words. I trust Kay knows what she's doing.

She slants her head and traces her finger along my chest, stopping to encircle a rigid nipple, before dropping down, all the way to my pubes.

"So wet," she hisses, as though she can't believe it, despite feeling it with her hand. She repeats the circle pattern: a wide one around my clit, before lowering the path of her hand again. Then, the lightest touch of a fingertip along my pussy lips. Again, but a bit more insistent this time. Two fingers slip-sliding along the wetness that has gathered there, for her.

Then, controlled, she slides in. Her eyes narrow a little when she does, and are mere slits by the time her fingers fill me. The intimacy of the moment breaks me down, and wetness now also pools in my eyes. I can't hide my tears from Kay, who looks straight at me, her head bobbing up and down slightly with her movements. I focus on the motion, on the determined set of her jaw, the lines bracketing her pursed lips, the crows' feet creasing her temples.

I'm filled with Kay. Only two of her fingers but it feels like so much more As if, by her penetration, she's giving herself to me—healing me. And the exhilarating sensation down there connects with all that's been going on in my mind and, for a blissful moment, extinguishes every flicker of self doubt. All the memories of all the events that brought me here—to her—are wiped from my brain. With every tiny, subtle movement of her fingers, she cracks through another one of the bricks in the wall around my heart. A wall I've been building since I was thirteen years old; perhaps earlier. She chips away at it by giving me pleasure. Not the pleasure I was used to with the likes of Thalia: carefully choreographed steps to take me to a semi-satisfying, polite climax.

The only reaction to the orgasm Kay is coaxing me toward is total physical and emotional surrender—as opposed to the grateful pat on the back I used to give

Thalia. As my pelvis takes over and moves toward her fingers of its own accord, more tears well in my eyes. Because I didn't just need Kay to fuck me. I needed her to make me understand that this is what she wants too. That I am whom she wants. I get the message loud and clear. It's in my heart. In my cunt. It's in her eyes when she shifts inside me, altering her course of action, adding another finger.

I'm so wide for her, open, on display. I don't need her to touch my clit and it's as though she knows that as well. She can read it on my face. I only need her to thrust deep inside of me, ravage me, destroy me a little to put me back together. My pussy lips strain around her fingers, and if I felt filled to the brim earlier, I feel Kay as a part of me now, giving me much more than the pleasure that is blasting its way through my flesh.

"Oh god," I holler, and, in the back of my brain, a different kind of voice says, 'I love you', but I wouldn't dream of saying that out loud.

I hold on to Kay for dear life, pulling her closer—and she lets me this time—possibly crushing her wrist in the process, because her fingers are still inside of me, still claiming me, still giving.

After I crash against the door, my limbs almost too relaxed to stand, Kay gently removes her fingers and stares at me for a while longer—the storm in her eyes has subsided, but I will remember what it looked like forever.

"Was that what you wanted?" she asks, a sly grin on her face.

"Fuck yes." I wipe a tear from my cheek and break out in a giggle at the same time. She slips an arm under my shoulder, keeping me upright and, finally, kisses me again. The kiss is slow and long, lingering and deep, and it's as though I can still feel her fingers inside of me as the afterglow of the orgasm pulses, spreading its warmth through me until it reaches the tips of my toes.

"Your turn," I say, when we break for air, our breasts still touching, the smell of my fluids all over Kay's hand.

Kay looks at me quizzically, the corner of her mouth drawn up. "Let's take a breather."

But I'm not having any of that. Kay is not someone whom I can enjoy sparsely, in measured doses. Somewhere in the back of my mind, I know that I probably should, that I shouldn't give in to this lure so easily—that it could so easily backfire again—but, looking at her, at the glowing sheen that has formed on her skin, and that irony-free glint in her eyes, I can't help myself.

"We should talk." She glances at me from under her lashes and the command of her voice is not powerful enough to convey her own conviction. "About Nina showing up."

"Later." My hands reach for the button of Kay's denim shorts. I have some unfinished business in there: I haven't tasted her yet.

"You're driving me crazy, Goodman." Kay's arm curves around my neck. "What am I going to do when you leave?" Her last words are barely a whisper, but my ears—always eager to pick up on anything Kay says—register them none-theless. They give me pause. In my mind, I've still only just arrived. I still have so much to work through, especially now with Nina's return. The thought of me going hasn't popped up once. It's a notion so far away, it doesn't exist for me yet. I have a wall to climb over first. A family to forgive. A sister to get reacquainted with. And, more than anything, a self in dire need of acceptance.

"I just got here." My hand freezes under the waistband of Kay's underwear.

"It feels like forever to me." It's the first time I recognize my kind of doubt in Kay's demeanor.

"Hey." I pull my hand from her panties and tug her close. "I feel the same way."

"Do you?" Kay takes my hand and drags me to the bed. "It hardly seems possible."

"Why?" When I feel put on the spot, I always react more bluntly than I want—another trait I share with my mother. "Because of why I came here?" If she holds it against me now, this ends before it has even started. I can't help my brain from going in that direction, my all-or-nothing streak taking over again.

"No, silly." She lifts up my hand and presses a kiss on my palm. Her own hand is so close to my nose, I can smell myself on her again. "Don't ever think that. Okay?"

I give a slight nod.

"Say it out loud. I need to hear it, Ella." The emphasis she puts on my name makes me sit up a little straighter.

"Okay." I'm useless in situations like this. Brain freeze. Possibly heart freeze.

"You're here on holiday. Northville is not your home. You're just passing through—regardless of the reason you came—you're not here to stay. I just…" Kay's voice breaks a little. "I'm not sure if I can attach myself the way I have to something so fleeting and temporary."

I can barely look at her, too aware that, once again, I've been too caught up in the turmoil of my own emotions to take Kay's feelings into account. The pressure to say the right thing at this very precarious moment makes my throat go dry, but I have to bite the bullet; I have no choice.

"While it is true that falling in love was so low on my list of things to do in Northville I didn't even consider it a possibility, I could never have guessed that I'd meet someone like you." I squeeze Kay's fingers between mine, desperately trying to hold on. "But now, sitting here with you, just being near you, I can hardly imagine what coming back would have been like if I hadn't taken a shine to Kay Brody. Seeing you again, from the moment I first laid eyes on you after all these years, has colored every single experience I've had here. Mainly in making some very hard things much more bearable for me."

"Glad to be of service." The sarcasm in Kay's tone is all new to me; and it does throw me—cuts straight through my flesh, settling as dead weight in the pit of my stomach.

"Do you really think I'd just walk away?" Without even thinking about it, I drop her hand.

"You have a life in Boston. My life is here." Kay clears her throat. The emotion is clearly getting to her as well. "No matter how strong this pull between us is—that moment we just had—it can only fade away with time."

I suck in a deep breath and find her eyes. "I'm the one with years of experience in negative thinking, Kay. It's sort of what I do. Think things to death. But, with whatever is blooming between us—and I think we both know what it is —my mind has not gone there once. Not even for a split second."

"Because you have a million other things to stress about." Kay doesn't let up. Is this some sort of test? Weaken my resolve by giving me an earth-shattering climax that ties me to her in ways previously unknown, to then launch an assault of gut-wrenching questions on me? "Do you remember what I told you about my father? That all he wanted for me was to be happy? I don't see a happy ending here."

Is this the same person who urged me to not overthink everything? Has the destructive power of fear gotten to her as well? Is it really that contagious?

"What are you trying to say?" I barely manage to squeeze the words out of my throat.

"I don't know." Kay shakes her head. "I think I've somehow fallen head over heels in love with you. With this person who, most of the time, doesn't even realize how bloody gorgeous she is. And I don't really know what to do with that. I'm afraid that you see me as some sort of rock, someone to hold on to and, once you make it through, once you've finished what you came here to do, you won't need me anymore."

"Could it be that," I start to say, putting a hand on Kay's shoulder, "you're just as afraid as I am?"

Kay gives a shy chuckle, draining a bit of tension from the room. "God, I'm being more lesbian about this than you."

I bump my arm against hers. "We all get caught up in the moment sometimes."

"You know what's craziest of all?" Kay's lips start to slip into that slow smile again. "That I went off on a rant like that while you were sitting on my bed completely naked."

Somehow, what has been said in the past five minutes humanizes Kay for me. After what just transpired, in my mind, she can no longer only be the person I turn to at West Waters when I want to cry, or confess, or feel better about myself. She's more than that now.

"That's wholly unacceptable." I start pushing her down on the bed, not waiting until her back has hit the mattress to find her lips with mine.

22

W hen, at last, I get rid of Kay's shorts, I still desperately want to delve my tongue between her legs and taste her for the first time, but it doesn't feel right in that moment. It feels like an action to be savored at a better time. Because, for all the blind lust that has gotten me here, naked in her bed, at the core of all this, it's not what defines us. What got us here is all that came before. Kay's kind smile. Her quiet, but persistent voice. Her gentle way with me and how she responded so solidly—like such a consistent presence in my life already—to everything I've told her.

So, instead of diving headfirst into that wave of lust again, into a moment that, perhaps, has come too soon, we lie under a single sheet in her bed. Both of us silent for several minutes, before I break the quiet that has settled around us—that is almost cradling me back to sleep.

"Can I sleep here tonight? Nina wants to stay at the cabin. I'm not sure it can take both of us."

"You're always welcome here. As long as you don't feel as if you have to spend time with me. I know you don't get to see her very often."

"Which is precisely why the two of us holed up in that cabin feels a bit too much like a Goodman family immersion."

Kay shifts on top of me, looking down at me from where she was lying in the nook of my shoulder. "What happened with Nina and Christopher Hardy?"

"First love gone wrong, I guess." I was fifteen, very aware of myself, but also quite clueless about what was going on around me at the time. "Nina and I weren't exactly close; she was eighteen and at the height of her rebellious teenage years."

Kay settles back on my shoulder. "Christopher was such a stunner back then. I know pretty much everyone in this town, but I have absolutely no idea what happened to him."

"Nina was so crazy about him, but, you know, in my parents' eyes he wasn't exactly a worthy suitor. Sort of a wrong side of the tracks situation. It didn't help that she carved his name into Dad's favorite deck chair, just to spite him." I push myself up a bit, trying to reconstruct the chain of events in my mind. "Ever since she was sixteen—after my dad's big revelation—Nina started hanging out with Hardy and his crew. They may have gotten in some trouble, but really, they were just teenagers like the rest of us. With a bit of a bigger mouth, maybe. And a slight attitude problem. I'm fairly certain they smoked weed and all of that, but, as far as I know, it was all quite harmless. But my parents just wouldn't have it. They couldn't stomach their oldest running around with the likes of Christopher Hardy.

"Mom went as far as to search Nina's room when she was in school, searching for anything that could serve as evidence in her quest against Christopher. One day, she found two bus tickets to San Francisco, and that's when the shit hit the fan.

"During the huge argument that followed—you can imagine how furious Nina was when she found out that

Mom had been going through her private stuff—it came out that Nina was planning to run away with Christopher. Harsh words were spoken. She was grounded, of course. The atmosphere in the house dipped to an all-time low, which is saying something considering the regular arctic temperature of everyone's mood in the Goodman family.

"But Dad couldn't leave it at that. You have to remember that he'd been struggling to regain Nina's respect for a few years by then—and Nina was never one to mince her words. She tried to diminish him every chance she got. She was at that age where, by default, parents couldn't do anything right, on top of the mistakes Dad had admitted to.

"In a rage—which should really be my family's middle name—Dad stormed off to the Hardys' house, told Christopher's parents all about Christopher and Nina's scheme to flee to San Francisco, and basically destroyed their relationship. Or, in Nina's words: her life."

Below me, Kay shakes her head. "She's been angry at your parents her whole life for that?"

"Well, among other things, but yes. I do understand to a certain degree. It was the final straw for her. When love is involved at that age, it always hurts a million times more. And I suppose, if our family had been just a tad less dysfunctional, she would have taken it like any other girl her age. Admitted defeat, sulked for a few months, and moved on. But things being what they were, she couldn't. After she left home not even six months later, which was, ironically, what Mom and Dad wanted to stop her from doing in the first place, she sent me a letter. It spoke of festering wounds, hurtful lies, lack of respect, an unacceptable, distant sort of parenting not fit for the age we lived in anymore, all those sorts of things." I blow some air through my nostrils. "It's just like my dad said the other day. Nina is just as stubborn and unforgiving as Mom." I rake my fingers through Kay's hair. "And, in the end, isn't that what it's all about? As much as we can't stand it, once we grow up, we see so much of ourselves in our parents. If you're lucky, what you see entails mostly good things, with a few annoyances thrown in for good measure because that's just the way it is, but in our case, Nina and I, all we see is failure to communicate, expressing love through judging and incessant meddling instead of just letting things play out.

"I should really only speak for myself, but, even when my mother says something completely reasonable, something with which, on a purely objective level, I can find no fault, it still irritates the hell out of me sometimes. Just because *she*'s the one saying it. And what right does she have to be that person now? This woman saying the right things, acting all reasonable, when all throughout my youth—when I could only see things through that narrow lens of intolerableness and insecurity—all I ever felt she did was put me, and everyone else, down."

"Nobody's perfect, Ella." For once, Kay's response seems completely inadequate. Possibly because this line of conversation—or, rather, my monologue—is getting me quite worked up.

"I know. Least of all me. One of the main sources of guilt is that I've always failed to feel thankful for what I did have. A roof over my head. Clean clothes to wear. A home-cooked dinner every night. According to the calculations I did in my head, at least fifty percent of all the children in the world were much worse off than me. Then why do I have the right to feel so screwed up? To feel so emotionally damaged?"

"That's not what I meant." Kay sits up to look at me intently. "You're perfectly entitled to any emotion you've ever had."

"Oh god," I groan. "Family is just so complicated. But

when I see the confidence kids have these days, I can't help but wonder where they get it. For some, it's their personality, but for most of them, it's how they've been brought up." I squeeze Kay's neck. "You're hardly a child, but look at you, Kay. Would you be this beautiful, strong, confident, always-holding-it-together kind of person if it hadn't been for your family and how they were with you? I'm not using the term 'raised' on purpose, because I strongly believe that when you have children, the most important thing to do is to lead by example."

"Every family's different, but none of them are free of burden."

"That may very well be true, but some will always be more toxic than others." My fingers stroke her neck. "Over the years, I've gotten somewhat of an eye for it. It only takes me a few practicums to figure out which of my students might have an overbearing mother or an absent father. And every so often, I see myself. A shy, retiring first-year biology student trying to adjust to life on campus. As much as college set me free, it was hardly an easy time for me either. To be thrown into this new world with zero confidence. Actually, no, I'm putting it wrong. To meet all these new people and discover that most of them had no problem displaying their personality and attracting other people just by being them-selves. My freshman year was hell."

A rush of air floats over my skin as Kay expels a sigh.

"What?" I push myself up a bit more.

"It could just have been your personality. You're shy. So are a billion other people on this planet."

I don't immediately reply. I try to picture Kay in college. What would she have been like in a place like that? I try to fit her into the categories of people I've made up in my mind. The ones I came up with in my early twenties, when I had nothing better to do than study my fellow students and come up with the theory that some personality traits seemed to be universal and always seemed to fit a certain type of person.

"I think, socially, you would have done well in college."

"Socially?" Abruptly, Kay's posture goes rigid. "As opposed to what? Intellectually?"

"What? No, I don't mean it like that, Kay. I'm not referring to that at all."

"Do you think I didn't get into college because of my intellectual capacities?"

"God no, absolutely not."

"Well then, you should work on the disparaging tone you use sometimes." Kay glowers at me. "Are you even interested in the real reason why I didn't go to college? Or are you too busy navel gazing and complaining about your privileged, but oh-so difficult life?"

"What the—" I barely recognize the kind, patient person I fell so hard for. Instinctively, I pull the sheet up to cover my naked flesh. Kay must have had the same idea, because we tug at the sheet at the same time and there's not enough of it to cover the sudden distance between us and our bodies. "I think I'd better go."

"Why?" Kay drops the sheet and gets out of bed. She stands there, illuminated by the midday sun slanting through the window, her skin bare, but holding no appeal to me. "Because running is what the Goodman girls do?"

Anger rises in me, the unstoppable fury I recognize from my youth, a ball of rage crashing through my flesh, obliterating everything. "I confided in you. I told you everything because I never, not for one second, believed you would hold it against me like this. I trusted you."

"Ella, listen to me." She sits back on the bed. "I'm not throwing anything in your face. The only point I'm trying to make is that a difference of opinion does not have to lead to an all-effacing argument."

"Difference of opinion?" I'm almost foaming at the mouth with rage. It's difficult to pull a sentence from the storm that brews in my racing mind. "I thought you understood." It's all I can say.

"Your sister, who didn't come back for anything else, came back for you. Both your parents are alive and, despite not being able to express it the way you want them to, they love you." She taps her chest. "*I* am here for you."

Trapped inside the red mist in my head, I can't possibly find a way to understand why Kay seems to have turned on me. "Fuck you," I scream, before trying to locate the few clothes I was wearing when I came here.

"Don't run." Kay's voice is firm enough to stop me in my tracks for a split second, but her hold on me seems to have disappeared already. A sense of utter betrayal rips through me. "Ella." She walks from behind the bed and positions herself in front of the bedroom door. "Stay."

"Why should I stay?"

"Because we're both only human." She crosses her arms across her still bare chest. "I may seem like this flawless creature to you, someone with infinite wisdom and patience who always says the right thing, but, just like you—just like your parents—despite doing my best with what I have, I fail sometimes." A lone tear dangles from her eye. "And today is the fifth anniversary of my mother's death, so excuse me if I can't listen as attentively while you go on about how your parents screwed you up."

"Oh shit." My clothes drop from my hands. "I'm so sorry." I walk over to Kay and, without thinking—or asking for permission—throw my arms around her. "I'm so so sorry."

"You didn't know," Kay sniffles into my ear. "I didn't mean—" Her words stall as she rests her head on my shoulder.

"Let's sit for a minute." I try to coax her toward the bed again, but Kay holds me in such a tight grip, I can't move.

"Will you come to the cemetery with me?" The fragile tone with which she delivers the words cuts right through me.

"Of course."

Kay eases her grip on me, starts to pull back. "I'm sorry. I'm usually not such a wreck about it."

"It's fine." I let my hands slide down her sides in search of her hands. "No apologies required. Remember?"

She nods, a pained grin on her lips.

I feel strangely privileged to see her this way, with her soul on display.

"Tell me what you need?" I'd do anything to have the light turn back on in her eyes.

"Go be with your family." A sterner note has crept back into her voice. "That's what I need, for you to be with them. To try."

"Okay." It feels as though some unknown sense of perspective has been unlocked, like the clouds have parted and a sudden, unexpected ray of sunshine is lighting up a spot that hasn't been illuminated for years. "When do you want to meet?"

"Whenever you're ready. Just come by the lodge. I'll be around."

"I can stay a while longer if you want."

"No. I'm fine being alone, Ella. I cherish it."

"Okay," I say again, but, although my replies may seem automatic, the fire in my heart is back at full throttle. I curl my arms around her waist again and look her in the eyes, before planting the most gentle of kisses on her nose.

23

A mixture of nerves, relief, and a strange sense of nostalgia wars inside of me as I pull up to my parents' driveway, Nina in the passenger seat. We were both silent on the way over here, sunk deeply into our own thoughts and predictions of how this afternoon might play out.

As soon as I slam the car door shut, a familiar head pops up in the kitchen's side window—as though someone in there is perpetually doomed to wait for a sign of another person's arrival.

"Fuck, Ellie," Nina says, leaning her elbow on the roof of my rental car for a moment, "I'm bloody nervous. Can you believe it?"

"Come on." I walk to the hood and extend my arm. Hand in hand—something we've never done since Nina turned twelve—we walk toward the back door of our parents' house. It opens before we have a chance to knock. My mother, her face as pale as the sheets she seems to always have drying on a line in the backyard, steadies herself against the wall while she stands there speechless. Of all the tears I've shed myself, the tears that brimmed in Kay's eyes this morning, and the ones that dangle from my dad's overly sentimental eyes at the most inopportune times, my mother's tears in this moment get to me the most. They seem to slice a piece of resistance right out of my heart.

"My girls," my mother mumbles, almost inaudibly. "Come here." She opens her arms wide.

As if drawn by a magnetic force, Nina and I inch closer, still holding hands, and fall into Mom's arms. As twisted as the thought sounds in my head, this moment would never have happened if I hadn't tried to take my own life. The embrace turns awkward quickly—not everything can be instantly resolved just by showing up—and our arms drop to our sides; the three of us shuffling our weight around, not yet knowing what to say.

"I'd better call your dad." Mom breaks the silence. "Guess where he is?"

We know this question doesn't require an answer and Nina and I exchange an eye roll before following Mom inside. As though unburdened of something already, we crash down on kitchen chairs while we hear Mom shout out Nina's return into the phone in the living room.

"He'll be here soon." Mom's voice has returned to normal. "Coffee?"

"Why don't I take care of that?" I rise, wondering if everything is still kept in the same spot. "Sit down, Mom." I sound like the caring, helpful daughter I always failed to be. I never even realized my own mother suffered from the same demons that brought me down—that I was, essentially, repeating her mistakes because, beneath it all, we are so similar.

"I've got it." I'm certain not wanting to sit and being served by me is a display of some sort of deep sentiment, but it doesn't matter. Both Nina and I are sitting in her kitchen, even I can feel the significance of that singing in my blood. I can tell—so easily—that Mom doesn't know how to deal with this fact just yet, but her life has suddenly changed dramatically. From having lost us both to being about to serve us coffee. I understand that she needs that moment with her back to us. Possibly to bite back tears—that outburst in front of us in the doorway must surely have been enough for her—or to just take another breath and let it register. Or, perhaps, to revel in that feeling of instant, pure happiness for a while longer, before we all have to start talking.

Within a matter of minutes, the three of us are hunched around the round kitchen table—still the same one we used to eat dinner at more than twenty years ago—steaming mugs of coffee in front of us.

I fully expect Nina to begin the conversation because, out of all three of us, she's the easiest talker. But my sister is uncharacteristically quiet. She gazes into her mug as if all the answers lay buried in the dark liquid it holds. That's when I know she's going to pieces. My news. The flight. Turning up on the doorstep of the house of her youth. Not even Nina's bravado is strong enough to withstand that storm of emotion.

"Tell me everything." The earlier brokenness in Mom's voice has healed already. I used to resent the steeliness in her tone—especially when used to downplay one of my accomplishments in school. Later, I theorized it must have been her way to make Nina feel better about not getting A's all the time. More than anything, I know it's how she hides herself —one of the many signs I missed because I was too busy creating my own mask of steel. "When did you get back?"

"This morning." Nina sits up a bit straighter. "Ellie e-mailed me last week and I, uh, just had to come."

Mom nods and, for a second, I expect everything to just be like it always was. After all, we've all become such experts at beating about the bush. "I've made a lot of mistakes."

There's still a trace of the familiar victimhood in Mom's voice—as though the mistakes she made were forced on her —but her tone is softer.

In the days before my suicide attempt, I used to lie awake at night, thinking of all the instances in my life when I had, completely by instinct, reacted to something in the exact same way my mother would, and vowed to take a pill for every single one of them.

Behind me, the door opens with a crash. I can't see him, but I can feel my dad's large physical presence in the narrow kitchen. I hear his breath being expelled rapidly from his lungs and, although this can only be imaginary, I hear his bones creak under the weight he carries.

"Where is she?" he booms, although, when I turn around, I can see him staring Nina straight in the face. His eyes are wet already. I quickly glance at my sister, who seems to be getting up in slow motion. I half expect her to give Dad a friendly jab on the arm, crack that smile of hers, but instead, she opens her arms and gives him a hug.

For all the tears that run down Dad's cheeks, he's not much of a sniffler. I always got the impression that he hated those outward signs of a sensitivity that never really befit him, that those inadvertent tears were not something he ever learned to hold back despite trying very hard.

Kay's words flit through my mind. *Your family loves you.* And I know that they do, but love isn't everything. I loved Thalia, and look how that turned out. I'm in love with Kay, but, being who I am, I was ready to walk out on her this morning.

After Nina left, in my eyes, my parents' love for both of us quickly translated into pressure on me. The one daughter that remained. Getting A's was never an issue, but choosing not to go to Oregon U was. All the hopes they pinned on me, albeit never spoken out loud, only drove me away further. Because I knew I'd never give Mom the chance to be mother of the bride. Or to have a brood of grand-children like her sister has. I knew I would never introduce my dad to a future son-in-law with whom he could talk about football and when to plant green beans in his garden—two subjects he could, ironically, easily have discussed with me, if we'd ever been on those kind of speaking terms.

Once Dad has sat down and Mom has poured him some coffee, the kitchen goes silent. I can't help but wish that Kay were here. She would know what to say. And I could use a supportive hand on my knee right about now. Because this sort of silence is what I've always hated the most. The kind that holds a thousand unspoken words, heavy with quiet reproach, deafening—and paralyzing—because of every-thing that can't be said.

It's okay to say you're sorry for what you've done. Dr. Hakim's words break through the fog in my brain at the right time for once.

"I'm sorry," I say, in my classroom voice—loud and confident and fake. "I'm sorry that what I did is the reason why we're all together here. I'm sorry to have put you through it." The rehearsed confidence has drained from my voice already. "I'm sorry—"

"It's okay, Ellie." Dad, who's sitting next to me, puts a hand on my arm.

"No, Dad, it's not." I remember the moment before the pills knocked me out. The immense relief that came with it —the exact opposite of what I'm feeling now.

"It's in the past now. The most important thing is that you're here." I can tell he's had a few beers, otherwise, words like that would never leave his lips.

"Why?" Across from me, Nina's face is covered in tears. "Why did you do it?"

"Give her a break, Nina." Mom's voice is harsh again, but Nina doesn't back down.

"If she can't tell us, what good is all of this? Or shall we just sweep everything under the rug again?" Nina's scolding glare roams across all three of us. "Shall we have some cake and pretend this is simply a long-awaited family reunion?" She fixes her gaze on me. "When my sister tries to kill herself, I want to know why."

"I don't need a break, Mom. We have to talk about this." I swallow hard. "It's why I came back."

"I just want to make clear that I, for one, don't require an explanation." Mom sighs heavily. "I'm fully aware that this family needs to have some difficult conversations, but this is not one of them." The look of compassion she shoots me is not one I've seen before—or, at least, not one I've ever chosen to remember.

"It's okay." For some reason, I too, feel compelled to break the unspoken no-unnecessary-touching rule of the Goodman family. I take my mom's hand in mine and squeeze it. "I want to explain." I suck in a deep breath and focus my gaze on a frame holding a picture of me and Nina when we were six and nine. "The reason why I chose not to live anymore was because I—" I stall because, in hindsight, the very reasons that seemed so clear to me at the time, are now extremely fuzzy around the edges, too undefined to be proclaimed out loud. And because any words I may manage to squeeze from my throat already sound invalid in my head. I feel small again, inadequate, a let-down. How I feel right now, facing my family, always feeling like I'm about to lose another battle in the war of the never-ending assault of my brain on my soul, is the reason why I did it. But I'm not exactly an expert at translating the carnage in my mind into understandable sentences.

I glare at the three of them and consider how their

mistakes have affected my life and, ultimately, my decisions, too. Two pairs of blue eyes and one pair of grey-green ones stare at me, waiting for some sort of deliverance, waiting for me to set them free with my words, and I may equally hate them and love them, and they may be my family, the same blood running through our veins—the same inadequacies testing us every day—but I don't owe them an explanation. Not for something I can barely explain to myself. Not for something that is beyond words. I acted. I shook the pills from the bottle. I wrote the letter. I cried for help and this is where it got me. This is where I am. Surrounded by my family, the people who made me, and who, I know this now, would walk on hot coals for me. And I wonder, when will it ever be enough? When will *I* be enough? I look into their misty-eyed faces, and I know this *is* enough. The four of us in Northville attempting a conversation. It's more than we've had for twenty years, possibly forever.

It's not perfect, but it's us. The silence that now grows is different, because I fill it differently. I used to only be able to crowd it with negative assumptions. *She's not saying anything because she's thinking this or that. Dad is silent because Mom looked at him that way. Nina broke all ties with us because we're a horrible family.*

What have you ever gained from being negative? Dr. Hakim has asked me about a million times. *When has it truly helped you?*

In this moment, my choice is to fill the silence that surrounds me with positive thoughts. They're here because they care for me. Nina came back because she loves me. What I did hurt them, but they're still my family, and I love all three of them no matter what. The bond between us *is* unconditional.

It doesn't matter how they perceive my silence. The only thing that matters is that, confronted with all three of them, I don't succumb to the guilt and the shame. I reject it. Because what Kay said is true: one mistake I made does not have to define the rest of my life.

"You did it because not living seemed like a better option than living with how you felt about yourself. Because, for some people, who have to drag themselves through slow hours of self-doubt and constant self-reprimand every single day, life is not a gift. You did it because you have an illness. An imbalance in your brain chemistry that you'll carry with you for the rest of your life. It wasn't weakness. It's who you are." Mom says it in words I would never have been able to find, let alone utter. My hand is still on hers and I dig my fingertips deep into her bony hand. "You're here and I couldn't be more proud of you."

On the other side of me, Dad has broken out in loud sniffles, shuffling in his chair.

"Oh fuck it." Nina rises and walks to my side of the table, placing a hand on Dad's shoulder in the process. She ruffles her free hand through my hair. "How about I pour us all something stronger?"

24

W hen Kay and I arrive at the cemetery the sun has already dipped behind the trees, bathing the grounds in a dreamy half-light that gives our visit an eerie quality.

With measured, sure strides she guides me to her family's plot. "Dad would never have forgiven me if I hadn't buried them together. Not that I believe in any of that life after death nonsense." She takes my hand and turns to me. "Which may make what I'm about to say sound extra ridiculous." Her grin has a solemn air to it, as if not wanting to go all out because of the place we're at. "Mom, Daddy," she turns to the gravestone again, gripping my hand tightly, "I'm sure you remember little Ella Goodman. She's grown into the brainiac professor we always thought she would be, but she's also much more than that. She's kind, a little too self-deprecating perhaps, funny and utterly stunning, and I've taken a bit of a shine to her. I hope you can approve." She turns back to me. "Mom used to say that I should spend more time with the likes of you instead of wasting my time fawning over your older sister. She would be so proud."

I'm a bit wobbly on my legs from the brandy I drank at my parents' house. I had to call Kay to pick me up after being declared unfit to drive by all three of my family members. All I can do is grin at her stupidly, my limbs loose from the alcohol, and my mind relaxed after our family reunion.

Kay slings an arm around my neck and pulls me close. "I do all right by myself, but I miss them so much." The seed of a crazy plan takes root in the back of my mind. It needs time to incubate before I can even really think about it, but it's there, pulsing like a faint neon light in my brain. "I'm sure they would be proud of you. What parent wouldn't be?" I lean into Kay's solid frame, her muscles hard against me.

Kay just nods, the set of her jaw strong, her teeth clenched together.

"Thanks for coming," she says after a while.

"Don't mention it." I feel like such a part of her life already. "What do you usually do on this day?" Even though my voice is quiet, it still echoes between the headstones, coming back to us as a ghostly whisper.

"Go to The Attic. Raise a glass to Mabel and Patrick Brody." Kay tugs me closer. "Will you join me?"

"Of course."

Kay's smile stretches wider this time. "Do you think it is in any way inappropriate to kiss you in front of their grave?"

I shake my head. Despite not being a religious person, the cemetery does give me pause. The air is different here, demanding respect for the dead. Out of nowhere, the thought hits me that I could have been lying here, buried in the soil of Northville.

"Show them that you're happy." My throat closes. Before my voice collapses completely, I find Kay's ear. "Show them that we're both happy to be alive."

———

When we arrive at The Attic, nerves fill me and I can't shake the preference of wanting to spend this evening on Kay's deck, perhaps with a skinny dip. But, at West Waters, with Nina's arrival, everything is different now as well. So I plant my behind on a bar stool while Kay orders us drinks.

"Let's go into a booth," she says after receiving two beers.

Relieved, I follow her into the booth I occupied with my dad the week before.

"What a day." Kay lifts her glass and clinks the rim to mine.

"How are you holding up?" It seems like weeks ago that we were lying in my bed at the cabin.

"I'm fine. Perhaps, emotionally, a bit more raw than usual." Kay extends her arm toward me on the table top. "By the time Mom died, she had suffered so much, it was almost a relief." She splays her fingers on the wooden surface. Instinctively, I reach for her hand. "The first time she got sick, I had just been accepted to UT. Literally, the day after I received my letter, she was diagnosed.

"Obviously, I couldn't go. I made that decision as soon as they told me she had cancer. To this day, I still believe that if I had gone off to college she wouldn't have pulled through that first time. But I stayed and she did pull through. Don't get me wrong; it was rough. Chemo is not pretty. But she made it through, went into remission, and was declared cancer-free for a long time afterwards.

"There was a lot of stress every time she had to go in for a check up, but we always had a party after. Until the day came when the news was bad again." Kay turns her arm on the table so her palm faces upwards. "She fought. God, Mom was such a fighter. She didn't give up until the end." Kay's fingers curl tightly around my wrist. "Her last words to me were, 'Sleep tight, my beautiful princess. See you in the morning.' She was so much stronger than my dad. It killed her that she had to leave him behind, as though she knew he would perish without her." She swallows hard. "And he did."

"I'm so sorry." Kay's strength is engrained in every little thing she does. It's in her body language—never wavering, always displaying purpose. My memories of Mrs. Brody are vague at best, but looking at Kay, taking in her grace and the determined stare of her eyes, I can see a little of Mabel Brody looking back at me.

"It's life, you know. People die. Nothing we can do about it."

"I'm sorry you missed out on college."

Kay just shrugs. "It probably wouldn't have been for me, anyway. I was always happy here. Never yearned for greater, faraway things."

"That's an illusion anyway." I think of my life in Boston. Do I miss anyone there? Does anyone miss me?

"Imagine me in Texas." A smirk slips onto her lips. "A biracial, bisexual woman who craves the outdoors and doesn't take shit from anyone. I'm also not someone who could thrive in air-conditioned rooms."

We both burst out laughing. Kay's eyes narrow to slits when she giggles. I want to run my fingers along the lines of her face. I want *her*. The beer is hitting me hard, making me feel how exhausted this day has left me, but I'm sure I can muster up the energy to make the thoughts in my head come to life.

Before I have a chance to propose continuing the night elsewhere, the door of The Attic flies open in a rush of wind and loud bouts of laughter. My dad, his arm around Nina's neck, followed by—I have to blink several times to clear my vision before I can actually believe it—my mother, walks in.

My father signals the barman. "Drinks all around, Joe. We're celebrating."

Perplexed, I glance at Kay, who shoots me a comforting smile. "More family time, I guess."

I duck out of the booth and catch Nina's eye. All three of them look as though they drained every last drop of that bottle of brandy we started earlier. A surge of panic in my blood. How can this possibly end well? Too much alcohol and The Goodmans have never mixed well. Mom and Dad's heads shoot up in my direction.

Quickly, I turn to Kay. "We *can* get out of this," I whisper.

Nina has reached our booth and throws her arms around me. After letting go, she eyes Kay and sends her a cocky grin. "Good to see you again, Brody."

I look at Kay expectantly, waiting for some answer— secretly praying that she'll give me an excuse to get out of there. She just blinks once and nods solemnly. "How are you settling in, Nina?"

"Scoot over." Nina pushes me back into the booth and presses her hip against mine.

"Drinks for my girls." Dad has sauntered over, Mom following close on his heels. Does she ever come here? I always believed she hated this place with a vengeance, that she thought of it as my dad's second mistress after he ended it with the first. Apparently 'my girls' includes Kay, as he deposits fresh beers on the table for all three of us.

"We must be interrupting," Mom says thoughtfully, nudging my dad in the arm.

"Nonsense." Kay shuffles further into the booth, freeing room on the bench for my dad. "Welcome, Goodmans."

On our side, Nina and I make room for Mom.

A few minutes ago, Kay and I were engaged in an inti- mate conversation and now my entire family is hunched around a table filled with beers. She seems so far away, perched next to my dad like that.

"Are you going steady now?" I can smell Nina's boozy breath as she asks the inappropriate question. Only this morning I told her that Kay and I had slept together for the first time. Perhaps jet lag and brandy erase short term memories.

"Nina!" Flashback to when I was fourteen and Nina caught me holding hands with Desmond Johnson.

"Your family sure seems fond of me," Kay says, her eyes on me, calming me down.

"I hear you own this place now." Nina has gone right back to being as annoying as she was as a teenager. Her remark also tells me that she and my parents must have been discussing Kay after she picked me up. "A woman of many trades… and persuasions."

Under the table—just like when we were children—I kick Nina hard in the shins.

"Ouch." She glares at me, her mouth drawn into an O. As though hurting the unexpectedly returned daughter is the biggest crime ever.

"Just shut the fuck up."

"Girls, jeez, it's like you never left," Mom blurts out. The flush on her cheeks betrays the ingestion of a few glasses of hard liquor as well.

"So, Nina, what have you been up to?" Kay asks in an even, conversational tone.

"She was an extra in *The Hobbit*," Dad chimes in.

As much as I want to revel in this moment of sitting amidst my estranged parents and my sister who eloped, engaging in meaningless conversation, the entire situation is already starting to drive me crazy.

"Must pay well." I can't help myself. "If that's all you've ever done all these years."

"We can't all be grade A students destined for greatness like you, Little Sis." There's snideness in Nina's tone, but not as much as I had expected.

"We're very proud of the pair of you," Dad says. My jaw almost hits the table as my mouth drops open with sheer disbelief, but it doesn't stop there. "No matter your professional or academic accomplishments."

Nina sits there, basking in some newfound daddy's girl glory, while, in the pit of my stomach, a knot so tight it will take many hours of therapy to undo it, starts building. Because, what I hear is: Ella may have worked her ass off while Nina was off somewhere gallivanting without frequently updating us on her whereabouts for years, but Ella tried to kill herself and Nina came back, which pretty much puts both of them at even keel. And I try. I try very hard to not think that way—in that destructive, going-nowhere fashion that sucks the joy out of everything—but it stings nonetheless. For all the degrees I've amassed over the years, in that moment, it still feels as though to them I will always be the daughter who attempted suicide. No longer 'their youngest', or 'the one living in Boston', but 'the one who gave up on life'.

As though the honor of such a compliment quickly becomes too much for Nina, she wraps an arm around my shoulder and squeezes tight. "I'm beginning to wonder why I ever left," she jokes.

And I'm beginning to wonder if I've somehow landed in some parallel universe, where my family's history has been magically erased, and we've always been a cheery, albeit borderline alcoholic family, going to the pub together, jesting like there's no tomorrow.

"Fuck this." The words start as a quiet hiss expelled from between clamped-together teeth.

"Language," my mother automatically says, only adding

to my bewilderment, but letting me know that I'm being heard in the process.

"Will this family ever snap out of its denial? What does it take? Huh?" Kay's hand snakes over the surface of the table, trying to reach my elbow, but I ignore it. "What does it take for you people to wake the fuck up? Nina ran away because you did what any parent would have done, and that makes you proud? Mom was depressed for years and no one ever bothered to tell me, which, for your information, might have spared us this whole ordeal."

"Ella," Kay says sternly, making me look up. "Don't say things you'll regret."

"Regret? I have nothing but regret. What's a little more added to the pile? Living with regret is basically what I do with my life. And you know why?" Little drops of spit have started to form at the corners of my mouth. "Because they were lousy parents. There, I said it. You were so shitty at it—"

"Enough." Kay has risen from her seat, her palms planted firmly on the table, her torso leaning over. "Take a deep breath. And stop talking."

My muscles collapse and I fade into the bench, wanting to disappear into the worn leather completely. Shame engulfs me instantly. The ugly side of me, this side of me that I always hate the most when I wake up in the morning—the part I wanted to extinguish forever—has taken over and I don't know where to look. Don't know how to undo the things I've said. Certainly, an apology will not suffice. The damage has been done, of that I'm sure. But what's worse, is that nagging feeling in my soul that, even though I should have been strong enough to avoid this outburst, the gist of it, in my ears, still rings true.

"I'm sorry." The same two words that started sounding inadequate when I turned twenty-one and chased away Amy, my first girlfriend, with too many of them. The same two words that would elicit the sort of ice-cold glare from Thalia that, perversely, turned me on like nothing else she ever did. The same words Kay has forbidden me to utter. "I'm sorry." I hold my hands up in defeat. "I shouldn't have said that. I know that, under the circumstances, you did the best you could." If only they hadn't walked into The Attic like a merry gang out on the town. *If only.* Sometimes in Boston, when looking out over the Charles River from my bedroom, taking in that sprawling, staggering view outside my window that should have lifted my spirits, but always failed, I would play the 'if only' game. *If only Dad hadn't cheated. If only Mom had found a way to be happier. If only Nina hadn't run away. If only I could deal with it better.*

'If' and 'only' are the two most useless words in the human vocabulary, Dr. Hakim had made a habit of saying. *They should never be used together in a sentence, because they speak of something that's beyond your ability to change. A waste of energy.*

What's his life like? I used to think, when he came out with one of his well-practiced phrases. *Does he really have it all so together as he makes it appear?*

"Ellie, it's fine." Dad is the first to speak. "It's important that you can say these things." Where did he all of a sudden go to shrink school? Or did someone whisper it in his ear while ordering a beer from Joe?

I shake my head. "It's never okay to say things like this. Never."

"So many things are not okay to say and do," Nina cuts in, her tone surprisingly light. "Does it ever really stop us from doing them? I don't think so." She taps her fingers on the table. "Would everyone have been better off if I hadn't been the hothead that I was and packed my bags? Perhaps, but who knows? Have I hurt Mom and Dad—and you, Ellie —by settling on the other side of the world? For sure."

I glare at her tapping fingers and she stops their movement.

"I've had a lot of time to think about this, and yes, we could go down your route. The difficult, painful one, because, let's face it, Ellie, you're a fan of the hard way through. Or, we could, slowly but surely, try to forgive each other for all the mistakes we've made and the hurt we've caused each other. None of us sitting here is innocent"—she glances at Kay—"except you, of course, Brody. Sorry to be dragging you into this."

Kay waves her off with that determined hand gesture she has.

"We could just go on with our lives, Ellie."

"Just like that?" I mumble. "It's that simple?"

"Of course not, honey." It's Mom's turn to speak, her voice so shaky it makes me tremble inside. "We are not the same people we once were and"—she halts here, taking her time to find the words—"you need to understand that we don't think any less of you because of what you did. It shocked us. It hurt us. It, frankly, made the bottom drop out from under our lives. But we love you just the same. You're ours, Ella. You're our beautiful, brave daughter. You always will be."

We burst out into tears at the same time—as though both looking into a time-machine mirror.

"This was never going to be easy." Kay's deep voice cuts through the ensuing silence. "But you have each other, and that's a lot."

25

In the car back to West Waters, Kay at the steering wheel, my sister—out cold—in the back, I sulk in silence, but rage on the inside. My quiet anger is, for once, not aimed at my parents, but at my sister who, just this morning, didn't have a good word to say about Mom and Dad. But I have no more fight left in me for the day. I just want to drop Nina off at the cabin and curl up into bed next to Kay.

"Sorry for ruining your commemorative drinks." Sideways, I glance at Kay. She keeps her eyes on the road, her face in the same stern expression.

"Hey, I'm up for a fun family outing with The Goodmans anytime." From the way she says it, I can't be sure if she's being sarcastic or if she actually means what she's saying. "Never a dull moment, I tell you that." She casts me a quick glance, and the sparkle in her eyes gives her away.

After we've put Nina to bed, we walk along the water to the lodge.

"Dip?" Kay asks. "It seems like forever ago."

"I'm exhausted." I'm already half-leaning against her. "I want you so much and I'm too tired to do anything about it."

"Pity." Kay runs her fingers through my hair. "I had plans for us."

"Don't tease me, please." I make my voice sound extra pleading.

"If I can't tease you, then what can I do?"

"Mmm, you can give me a neck rub, or a back massage," I joke.

"Okay." Kay doesn't protest. "I can do that."

I lean a bit more into her, deeply inhaling her scent, and the pure air around us.

"If you do something for me as well." Kay intensifies her hold on me, her fingers pushing into my side. "I know that, on the inside, you're still fuming. Do yourself a favor and give your sister a break."

"Not you as well." I recognize my tone. Catty. Tight.

Kay stops. We've almost reached the lodge. Only a few more feet and I can shrug off my clothes, slip between Kay's cool sheets, and forget about this day.

"Listen, Ella." She positions herself in front of me, her hands on my shoulders. "You have to realize that not everything someone else says or does is an attack on you. People act for various reasons and, mostly, those reasons have far less to do with us than we like to presume."

"It's 'us' now, is it?" More poison coming from my mouth.

"You have to drop the defensive act. If you want something good to come out of your return home, you have no choice." She stares at me, her eyes as ink-black as the night sky. "If you want 'us'"—emphasis where I didn't expect it —"to have a chance, you need to let your guard down. And stop feeling so ganged up on, as though the entire world is against you, because, let me assure you, that silly notion only exists in your head. Nowhere else."

"It's just," I start, tapping into the last ounce of energy burning away in my body, "the way they were sitting there, as though Nina leaving didn't matter anymore, after all those years—"

Kay tilts her chin, lightly shaking her head. "You don't know what they talked about after you left. You can never know what goes on in another person's mind, Ella. Stop wasting your energy on trying to predict someone else's thoughts. It's as pointless as it gets."

Perhaps falling in love with someone like Kay is exactly what I needed. Someone I have a sizable emotional invest-ment in who actually makes me register the things she says, as opposed to just acknowledging them, hearing them briefly, the sound of the words sitting in my ear for a moment, before falling away because I always know better. How could I not? It's always been this way, ever since I can remember. This is how I've lived my life. Gauging other people. Filling in the silence. The little bit of confidence I do have, built with the wrong bricks. But mainly, through the years, ever since I first spotted that cold hard glare in my mother's eyes when she looked at my dad—sometimes even at me or Nina —I've been afraid of everything.

"Come on." Kay curves her arm around my shoulder again. "Enough therapy for you for one day." Slowly, we head toward the lodge, this haven of escape, this place where Kay and I originated—where she fucked me against her bedroom door.

"Were you planning on majoring in psychology at UT?" I ask as Kay unlocks the door.

"No, silly." That sparkle in her eye again. "Engineering."

I chuckle, releasing some of the tension coiling beneath my stomach.

"How about I draw you a bath?"

"If I believed in some deity in heaven," I clasp my hand solemnly to my chest, "I'd be sure he or she sent you to Earth especially to save me." I grab Kay's wrist and pull her close. She has that glint in her eyes again. From the way she hesitates to reply, I can tell she wants to say something I may not want to hear—again. "It's okay. As long as you draw me that bath, you can say it."

"Just one more thing." She inches closer, a mere inch of space left between our bodies. "I watched you interact with your family tonight, and I know you're someone who doesn't like to say things out loud. You prefer to let them fester until they burst out of you, the words tumbling out of you in an explosion of poison. One of the first things my dad taught me was to not go to bed with thoughts that bothered me. When I was little, he made me say them out loud while he tucked me in. There's so much power in saying something out loud, Ella, before it has the chance to turn sour. So, from now on, when you spend the night in my bed, let's do the same. Before you go to sleep, you need to give me a list of all the things that bothered you that day."

"That should make for some special pillow talk."

"And none of those wisecracks either."

"Or what?"

"I'm serious, Ella. If you want to be with me, you have to make an effort."

"I'm sorry." I lean my forehead against hers. "Deal."

With her index finger, Kay lifts up my chin. "Good." Her entire face smiles at me, eyes included. "Now go take off your clothes."

———

The bathroom of the lodge is old-fashioned, pale orange tiles from the eighties on the walls, cupboards that don't close properly underneath the sink. But it doesn't matter, because I have my eyes closed, the back of my head leaning against the edge of the tub, my body surrendering to the hot water, not an inch visible from underneath the mountain of foam piled on top of me.

Despite being so tired I can barely think, my mind goes there. Kay's fingers. This morning. And the look in her eyes when she slipped them inside. Without thinking, I let my hand wander down, the memory of Kay's fingers an irresistible turn-on.

"Why don't you let me take care of that."

Startled, I open my eyes and see Kay standing in the doorway, her body slanted against its wooden frame, a smile on her lips so seductive it takes my breath away. Kay doesn't wait for my response. With light footsteps, she crosses over to the tub and positions herself on the edge, disregarding the foam and how wet it will leave her clothes.

Under water, her hand finds mine—stopped in its tracks —and above, her eyes lock on me. In them, I see her desire for me glimmer with unmistakable fierceness, and that lust, for a moment, erases everything else from my mind. The way Kay wants me, how she can't hide it, how it's all over her face right now. It has the power to mend at least some of the wounds in my soul left by years of insecurity and doubt.

The water splashes softly around Kay's arm and, already, I'm spreading wide for her, my knees knocking against the sides of the tub, my pelvis floating on a bed of water, reaching up for her.

The tension of the day seems to have gotten to Kay as well. The path her finger takes is clear, not allowing for distractions, going straight for my clit.

"I want you to come for me," she says, a hint of something in her voice I can't place. Desperation or demand? "Once now and once later."

Her words may as well be a thrust of three fingers inside of me, that's how much they make my pussy contract—but Kay doesn't give me that satisfaction. Not yet. Instead, the meaty part of her finger is insistent on my clit, applying pressure under water, which creates an entirely different sensation than this morning, when she made me come at her fingers for the very first time. She circles her finger with the confidence of someone certain of the fact she'll get what she came for. Someone so solid in the knowledge that she can tip me over the edge with just a few tiny flicks that, just the sight of her, the set of her jaw and the self-assuredness in her eyes, is enough. With Kay, there's no room for questioning. If she wants it to happen, it will happen. In that, I'm hers.

"*Now*, Ella." The insistence of her finger has made its way into her voice, in her eyes, as she demands my pleasure, and I know that this climax is only half due to what her hand is doing under water. The other half, the most satisfying, core-shattering half of it, happens because of us. Because of this unexpected change of air between us. Because of how she talks to me. Because of what we have together.

"Oh." I clasp my hands around the edge of the tub, holding on as my body disappears under water. "Oh fuck."

When I open my eyes, the satisfaction is visible on Kay's face. Reassured of the power she has over me, she cocks her head and blinks once. "That was number one."

My limbs no longer feel as though all they want to do is sink into a soft mattress and rest. I can't wait for number two.

Kay stands and picks a towel off a rack next to the door. She opens it wide, indicating she has no plans to wait long to make me climax for the second time. Once I'm wrapped in the towel, she presses herself against me and leans in for a kiss. *I still haven't tasted her*, I think, when our lips meet. With the way she seems to love bossing me around, I wonder if I ever will.

"Go into the bedroom," she says, when we break apart. "Don't fall asleep. I'll be right there."

I hear the sound of splashing water as I make my way into Kay's bedroom and, still snugly wrapped in the towel, fighting against sleep after the climax and the warm bath, lie down. Against my will—because I want what Kay has in store for me much more than sleep—I can feel my body go limp the instant I touch down on the bed. *Emotional fatigue is just as draining as the physical kind*, Dr. Hakim once said. I now know what he means. Everything that has happened today flashes in quick pulses through my mind. My fingers inside of Kay. Nina's arrival. The burn of the whiskey. Kay's fingers inside of me. Bringing Nina home. The cemetery. The Attic. The bath tub. One more lazy blink of my eyelids, and I'm drifting off—ready to give my tired brain the time to digest.

"What did I tell you?" The stern quality in Kay's voice startles me awake. She saunters closer. "You can sleep all day tomorrow if you want, but tonight, I need you to be mine." The way the word 'need' comes out, indicates a desire I haven't yet seen in Kay. Maybe it's how she deals with overly emotional days, with the memory of loss, and grief. Maybe she really does need me to belong to her.

It's hardly a chore for me to blink myself fully awake. Kay has stripped off her clothes and her skin smells freshly washed. We've cleaned the day off us. It's time for the night.

"Sit up." Need and tenderness do battle in her voice, and it's exactly that blend that grips me by the throat—that would make me do anything for her. The towel falls off as I push myself up.

A darkness builds in Kay's eyes. A need so great it frightens me a little, but not as much as it exhilarates me. "I'm going to make you come and you're going to watch."

She turns her head away and looks into the mirror that hangs on the wall across from the bed. "I need you to see." With her hand, she pats the spot next to her, indicating where she wants me.

I shuffle over, a fresh burst of energy flaring in my muscles.

"Spread your legs." Kay's voice is shot to pieces by emotion, reflecting perfectly how I feel inside.

I let my knees fall to either side, exposing myself to the room, to Kay, and the mirror. Kay sits next to me, her body glued to mine in a sideways position, one hard nipple poking into my upper arm, her rasp of a voice in my ear.

"Look at yourself," she commands.

I glare at myself in the mirror, hesitantly at first, so self-conscious I want to avert my eyes. I see two women intertwined, Kay's hand caressing my inner thigh, half of her body covering my side. I stare into the blue of my own eyes and the dullness that used to greet me, cold hard morning after cold hard morning, is no longer there. I see fire, lightning, and love.

"Follow my hand with your eyes." Kay's voice has gone very quiet, but her lips are on my ear and every word registers loud and clear.

I lock my gaze on the motion of her hand. It trails upwards, closer, and I can't help but look at my own glistening pussy lips. A strange sensation takes hold of me, a foreign sort of arousal, the excitement of a new discovery saturating my blood. This arousal is not triggered by looking at my own intimate parts, but by Kay's approaching fingers. Two. Feather light on the sensitive skin of my inner thighs. Barely touching me, but inching closer.

"Watch me fuck you," she whispers, and it's enough to make my breath stall in my throat in a hiccup of excitement.

First, she spreads my pussy lips with two of her fingers.

Every vessel in my body seems to be pumping blood toward my clit, toward where Kay's fingers are headed—as though as much of me as possible wants to greet her there.

"Jesus," I groan, when the tip of one finger slips inside of me. I'm so wet, I barely feel it, but my eyes are witness to it, and the recruitment of a different sense sparks immediate pleasure in my flesh.

I watch as more of Kay's finger disappears inside of me, her arm crossing the pale skin of my upper body, the contrast of it making me see much more than how she fucks me. I see two women in this mirror: one giving, one receiving. And, although it's Kay's finger sliding deeper inside me, the ragged whoosh of her breath in my ear, how it stops and starts in sync with the motion of her hand, tells me that, to her, giving equals receiving.

Kay adds another finger, two digits parting my pussy lips in the mirror in front of me, but I'm distracted by her moans in my ear, by how they get interrupted by speech as she starts to say something. "I—" she begins, but doesn't finish.

"Say it," I hiss between my teeth, between the bucking of my pelvis, between the bursts of pleasure igniting between my legs. "Tell me."

"I'm so in love with you." I can barely make out the words through her breathy sighs and the sounds now emanating from my own mouth, yet, they've pierced my flesh and lodged themselves in my heart already.

As though saying it needs to be countered by upping my pleasure, Kay adds another finger. My eyes seem to go as wide as my pussy spreads for her. Kay's words in my ear, her fingers in my cunt, working me, finding something inside of me—just like, when I arrived at West Waters, she saw something in me I had failed to see for years.

Kay doesn't have to ask me to come this time. With part of her buried so deep inside of me, while her body embraces me, and her face is so close to mine, I'm there without demands needing to be made.

"Oh fuck," I stammer, again, for the second time in the past hour, as the pleasure crashes through my flesh, paralyzes my muscles, and surrenders my soul to Kay Brody. Exhausted, I let my torso fall against Kay's chest, but still, I can't keep my eyes off that woman in the mirror. The one with the wild eyes, with the look of freedom on her face. Me.

Kay leaves her fingers inside of me, copping a good look at herself. Our eyes meet in the mirror, both of us misty-eyed and satisfied. Then, slowly, she retreats, leaving me empty there, but filled with all of her in my head.

"Oh christ," I mutter, after dropping onto my back on the mattress.

Kay is quick to drape her body on top of me, her arm wrapped around me, one leg, bent at the knee, resting on my thighs.

"Now you can sleep," she whispers, but sleep is the last thing I want to do.

"Funny." I giggle, my breath on her cheek. "I'm not tired anymore."

"Really? After that, I thought I would have worn you out."

Suddenly, I feel as though my time with her has become overly precious. That I've wasted it on the wrong actions and emotions. And then there's that thing I've wanted to do to her since this morning—as much for her as for myself. I need to taste her.

"It's going to take a lot more than that to keep me away from where I want to go right now." I start sliding myself from underneath her.

"You won't hear me complain." Kay looks at me from below. Strands of hair have come loose from the ponytail she always keeps so tightly pulled back.

I lift myself on top of her, my entire body covering hers, and kiss her. For all the orgasms I've had since we arrived at the lodge, we've exchanged very few kisses. My knee dipping between her legs, I plant my lips on hers over and over again, exploring her mouth, letting my tongue roam free the way I want it to roam elsewhere in a few minutes.

When I push myself away from her to start my descent, she has a funny, eyebrows-scrunched-together look on her face.

"What?" I ask.

"You come so easily," she says. "I've rarely seen that in a woman."

A chuckle unleashes in my throat. "Only with you."

She nods, indicating that she understands the gravity of this, acknowledging that she knows that, with her, everything is different.

I kiss her again, our lips barely parting—tongues barely touching—and the image of her fingers disappearing inside me hits me again, sending a hot shiver up my spine. I feel Kay's wetness on my knee.

When I begin to fold my body, aiming my mouth in the direction it wants to go, Kay whispers, "I'm so hot for you, Ella." Another ripple of lust running across my back. Any remnant of exhaustion after this marathon day dissolves in the solemn silence that follows after her words. For an instant, I find her eyes again, gazing deep into the wild blackness of them, and they tell me everything I've ever wanted to hear.

Spurred on by Kay's words, I kiss my way down, inhaling her as I position myself between her legs. At last we meet, I think, looking down on the evidence of exactly how much she wants me. Puffed up lips, swollen into a dark red shade, her clit engorged and ready.

I kneel before her, as though she's the altar at which I

worship, and slip my hands underneath her behind. I start slowly, tentatively, licking along her lips, but soon, Kay's hands are in my hair, guiding me to where she wants me. As much as I want to teach Kay and her bossy ways a lesson, now is not the time. I follow her unspoken command and let my tongue dart around her clit.

"Oh yes," she moans instantly, and the sound of her sigh cuts right through me, but I don't give in that easily.

I slip the tip of my tongue between her wet, wet lips and drag it along the length of her, stopping, at the top, with another quick flick over her clit.

"Christ, Ella." The raw need in Kay's voice is so great, I don't have it in me to ignore it anymore. Still, I take the time I need to revel in this moment, in the joy of pressing my nose into her hair, in touching her this way, in having her give herself up to me. And if my mouth wasn't otherwise engaged, I'd say it too. I'd tell her how crazy I was about her, seconds before making her come, just to make the point extra clear.

Instead of saying it, I show her, by giving her exactly what she wants. I let her clench her fingers onto my skull, strands of my hair twirled around her palms. I let her coax me, let her take control.

Yet, the only body part truly in control of everything, is my tongue. It dances along her clit as Kay goes rigid beneath me, her hands clasped onto my head.

"Oh… God…" she exclaims, but I keep licking because I don't want to stop, don't want *this* to stop.

"Enough, enough," Kay begs for mercy, pulling my head up.

Her face is a mess of tears and bliss, a wonky smile on her lips, a glossy sheen of sweat on her skin.

I stretch out my body and move over to her, my face close to hers. I still smell her, her arousal is still everywhere. I realize she hasn't tasted me there yet either, and, if we wanted to, we could do this all night long, and all day tomorrow, and for the remaining time of my stay. But the fatigue returns, crushing me so much more than before. We have time, I think, as my body sinks into hers, my head on her shoulder, her arms around me.

I fall asleep within seconds.

26

"Morning." When I wake up, I feel as though I haven't moved an inch during the night, my body receded into the depths of sleep so far, rolling over wasn't even an option. But my head is no longer on Kay's shoulder. Instead, half of my face hidden in the soft pillows she uses, I look into her sleep-drunk eyes, blinking.

"Hey." Instantly, a wide smile conquers my lips and a giddy feeling takes root in my stomach.

"Do you want to take a bath?" she asks, a goofy smirk plastered across her face.

I can't help but giggle the way I did when I was a teenager and Nancy Moore came within a ten feet radius of my personal space. So this is what it feels like, I think, to wake up to love. "Maybe just a shower."

"Don't forget to check yourself in the mirror afterwards." Kay seems awfully pleased with herself.

"You." Under the sheet, my hand reaches for her, finding the warm skin of her belly. "You're such a top."

"Is that a problem?" She cocks up one eyebrow.

Is it? Ever since yesterday, it feels as though anything I did before, even with women I had fallen so in love with, holds no importance anymore. As though a new benchmark has been set. The slate wiped clean. "No." I shake my head, almost shyly.

"Either way, you were plenty versatile last night."

"Yeah right." I shuffle closer toward her, my body drawn to her again.

"What's on the agenda today? Nina time?" Kay cradles me in her arms and I inhale her sleepy morning scent.

"Oh god," I groan. "I can't bear to see my family today."

"Then don't." Kay says it in the most matter-of-fact tone.

"But she came all this way."

"Doesn't mean you have to be joined at the hip. Nina's a big girl. She can find her way around."

"Mmm." I nudge my nose against Kay's neck. "What do you propose we do all day?"

"Bathe." Kay kisses me on the scalp, and I feel the heat of her lips travel all the way through me.

"You're bad."

"I meant swimming in the lake, obviously." She gives her deep rumble of a belly laugh, and the sound of it is already so familiar to my ears—so distinct and comforting—I can't imagine life without it. "You're the one with impure thoughts."

I give her a gentle swat on the bottom, and it only makes her laugh harder.

"I have some stuff to do today, but feel free to stick around here if you don't want to go back to your cabin."

"Thanks." I relax back into the crook of her shoulder, and there's that thought I had yesterday at the cemetery again. Since it took root in the back of my mind, it has steadily worked its way forward, to the point of no return.

———

"There you are." Nina saunters toward me while I sit reading the Northville Gazette on Kay's deck.

Where I'd expected to feel a certain sense of deflation—and sisterly duty to entertain her—upon seeing her, her sudden appearance has an instant calming effect, as though my nervous system recognizes her from the years spent together in our youth. She's family and my subconscious will never forget.

"Join me?" I shield my eyes from the midday sun with my hand and glare at her.

"Why of course, Little Sister." She takes a seat in the chair next to me. "You're positively glowing today. I'm guessing Brody has something to do with that. Did she"—she makes a suggestive motion with her hips—"all night long?"

I swat the paper toward her. "Must you be so crass?"

"Where I live, this is how we talk, Ellie. I mean it, you really have to come visit me. Soon."

"I will," I say, and I mean it, too.

"So, what are you going to do about the old Kayster when your leave is up? Break her heart? She's absolutely smitten with you, the biggest fool can see that."

"Jesus, Nina. We've only just got together." *And I haven't even had the chance to pour you a drink before you ask me the hard questions.*

"So? I know you, Sis. Tell me what you're thinking."

"What I'm thinking is that I want to stay here with Kay forever."

"You'd move back to Northville for her?" She clicks her tongue. "She must be really spectacular in the sack then."

I roll my eyes, ignoring Nina's comment, but thinking about the future nonetheless.

"What's gotten into you, anyway? The way you were chatting with Dad last night as though you'd never even left? It didn't look like the same Nina who turned up on my doorstep earlier that morning."

She brushes one of her long blond curls out of her eyes. "Well, I was a bit tipsy, but…" She sighs and stares out over the lake. "He's my dad, Ellie. I only have one. Just like I only have one mom and one sister." Her voice tightens. I can almost hear her throat closing up. "All these years, I believed that, sometimes, despite being family, it just doesn't work. On my travels, I've met enough people who shared the same experience—most of them running from something family-related. But what you did, I guess it changed me too, or at least my perception. When I walked into that house yesterday afternoon, something inside me gave. The exact same thing that has kept me from coming back for so many years… it just broke, went to pieces, dissolved." She pauses to wipe a tear from her cheek. Before continuing, she holds up a finger. "We have one life, Ellie. And it's fucking precious and I no longer want to waste mine hating my family over some-thing that happened so long ago and that, quite honestly, I've blown so out of proportion, I could never get around it in my head."

I try to hide the tremor in my voice. "Moving back to Northville as well, are we?"

"I wouldn't go that far, unless Kay has any hot cousins she'd like to introduce me to." Nina reaches for a stray napkin lying on the table. "Fuck it, Ellie. Look at us." She shakes her head. "It's just that, the longer you stay away, the harder it is to come back."

"I know." I look at my sister, at the tears in her eyes, and, despite her wet cheeks, I can't help but smile. "I never asked you when your return flight is."

"I don't have one. I booked a one-way ticket. Your e-mail

didn't go into too much detail. I didn't know what state you were in." Another tear dangles from her eyelashes. "God, Ellie. I'll never forget that moment when I read those words."

"I'm sorry." I still feel shame, but it's less present. It feels more like a sentiment I can deal with. Not just because I'm sitting on Kay's deck, in her chair, drinking a Sprite from her fridge, but mostly because the past few days, something inside of me has shifted. Not thanks to Kay, or Nina, or anything my parents have said, but because of me. Because of the woman I saw in the mirror last night, and how she looked back at me, with a glint of hopeful happiness in her eyes. "Thank you for coming."

"I blamed them, you know. It was the first thought that crossed my mind. Then I blamed myself, for leaving you alone with them in that ghastly, cold house, to sit through those endless mute suppers." More tears. Nina doesn't even bother to wipe them away anymore. "Can you imagine my shock at seeing how they are together now? Like they've finally grown into a coat that was too big for most of their lives. It will never really fit, but it'll do. That's the impression I get. That they've settled for each other, because it's how it has always been, and with that, they've finally learned to understand and even appreciate each other to some degree."

"You're absolutely right." I sit there, under a glorious midday sun, realizing that there's no other person on this planet who understands me in the way that my sister does. "I've missed you, Nina. Even though, once past sixteen, you were such a royal pain in everyone's ass, I've really missed you."

"Hug?" Nina glares at me suspiciously. "That's really something I've learned to do in New Zealand, let people hug me."

"I think the occasion calls for it." I rise from my chair

and open my arms. Nina walks into my embrace and, our arms thrown around each other, we cry some more.

"Does Kay have any beer in that fridge?" Nina asks when we break from our hug.

"Of course." Grateful to spend a few minutes alone inside, I head to the kitchen. On the cabinet next to the fridge, there's a framed picture of Mabel and Patrick as I remember them. I pick it up and carry it outside with me, along with two beers. "Remember them?" I ask Nina.

"God yes. I used to fantasize they were my parents." Nina says it with a benign smile on her face. "Let's get real, Ellie. Dee and John Goodman are our parents and, well, we love them, but they'll never be our favorite people in the world to spend time with."

"You'll never be my favorite either, but I love you too." I clink the neck of my bottle against hers. "I think you should stick around for a while."

"Maybe I will, Little Sis, maybe I will." Nina tips her head back and swallows a large gulp of beer. "God, this lake. It used to feel like the only place where we were truly a family. Do you know what I mean?"

Strangely, I do. I nod and let my gaze wander. Because my head is filled to the brim with her, an image of Kay, naked and dripping, pops up in my mind.

"Remember when we were little and I used to push you in?" Nina snickers. "Before you learned how to swim. You were wearing these ugly orange things around your arms, so I knew you wouldn't drown."

"I hated you so much."

"It's what sisters do, Ellie. The way of the world and all that." Nina looks away from the lake and fixes her gaze on me. "Can you promise me you won't do it again?" Her eyes go misty as she asks the question. "I need to know. It's killing me inside. This giant worry. It sits here"—she taps her chest —"and I don't know what to do with it."

My eyes fill with tears as well, and I look longingly at the lake, wanting to jump in, to erase these tears I have to keep on shedding for what I did. But for the first time, I feel I can make the promise. "I won't." I reach out my hand and my sister takes it in hers.

EPILOGUE

"Pass the sauce, please," Dad says, and Nina, sitting next to him, cheerfully hands him the pot. It's the last night before I have to go back to Boston, and my family has gathered at the lodge, upon Kay's and my invitation.

During the Oregon fall and beginnings of winter, Nina's skin has lost most of its tan, and it looks as though she's gained some weight, but she's still here, and that's what matters. She still hasn't booked her return ticket.

"I need to make up for lost time," she told me when I quizzed her about it a week ago. "I can't just leave again." I knew exactly how she felt.

"I have an announcement to make," I say, once everyone is settled with a satisfying plate of Kay's pot roast in front of them.

"Oh my god, you're pregnant," Nina chirps, because she just can't help herself. I give her the evil eye while Kay clears her throat solemnly, indicating, to my ignorant sister, that this is an important moment.

"When I go back to Boston, I'm going to resign. I'm

going to sell my house, and move back here." My hand finds Kay's on the table. "Kay and I are moving in together."

"I knew you'd be renting that U-Haul." Nina again. This time, my Dad slaps her around the head playfully.

"That is truly wonderful news." Mom clasps a hand in front of her mouth. "I'm really happy for the both of you." I still can't get used to this sight, but my dad throws an arm around her shoulder and gives her frame a quick squeeze.

"We can do more processing while we eat," Kay says, "before it gets cold."

I'm not that hungry. Not out of nerves, but because of pure giddiness. I'm shacking up with Kay Brody. Although, technically, I moved in after Nina arrived. I'll be living at West Waters. I'll try to get a transfer to Oregon U, although chances of that are slim. If all else fails, I can teach biology at my old high school—or, perhaps, just run West Waters with Kay.

"You're not getting any younger," I told her. "You could use the extra pair of hands."

"I know exactly where I can use an extra pair of hands," she replied, before toppling me over on her bed and topping me again.

I think I decided that my time in Boston had ended a few days after my first night with Kay. No matter how many times I went over it in my head, the option of me leaving her behind for a long-distance-relationship and going back to my fractured life in Boston could only be perceived as a huge obstacle for my happiness. And happiness is what I'm all about now. Obtaining joy from simple things, like seeing Kay's face first thing in the morning: simple, but oh so powerful. Like casting my gaze over the now ice-cold lake and day-dreaming about jumping in naked with Kay when the temperature rises. Like lounging on the porch of our cabin with my sister, a fire crackling in the pit, and listening to her bohemian tales of being an extra on movie sets and—although I can't conjure up images of this, no matter how hard I try—sheep herding, rolling my eyes every time she uses a curse word.

"Now you'll have to give me father-in-law perks at The Attic, Kay," Dad jokes.

"Sure, John," Kay smirks good-naturedly. "Anything to keep you happy." I look at my dad, and how he so easily interacts with Kay, and I know that if it hadn't been for him —and for the sacrifices he made—this family would have fallen apart long ago.

I feel Mom's eyes resting on me, a sensation that once made my skin crawl. I look up into her version of a smiling face. It's more of a grimace that's painted on her lips, as though, throughout the years, she has lost the power to smile altogether, but it's a valiant effort.

"What?" I ask.

Before speaking, she pulls her lips into an even wider almost-smile. "I was just thinking about that time when you were ten years old and you put a pair of bunched up socks in your shorts, going around telling everyone you were a boy now."

"Oh jeez," I groan, "not that tired old story again."

"Please elaborate, Dee." Amusement glows in Kay's voice.

"Please don't." I shoot Mom a smile nonetheless.

"Oh come on, Ellie." Of course, Nina has to chime in. "You so wanted to be a boy back then."

"I just thought it was unfair that boys got to pee standing up and that, a few years later, I had to wear a bikini top when coming to West Waters. That's all."

"You were already such a lez back then." Nina shakes her head. "As if that Julia Roberts poster on your wall didn't make that clear enough. I'm surprised you even had to come out at all."

What the hell would you know? I want to ask. *You weren't here for any of that.* But I ignore my initial instincts, because, I've mellowed toward Nina too. My new-found zen philosophy doesn't work every day, but it helps to have Kay around. Just by being by my side, she reminds me that not everything is black and white.

"Life is not all or nothing," she said once, after I'd come back from another emotional visit to my parents, "learn to navigate the in-between areas. There are highs and lows, but there's so much more in between. Take me, for instance. Right now, I represent a massive high for you, but it won't always be that way. Life will throw things at us and, instead of letting them drag you all the way down, together, we will make it through."

"God, you're cheesy," I replied, before kissing her for a very long time.

"And you've become so mouthy. Must be all that hanging around with Nina."

Having Nina around has helped. Just to sit next to someone who understands things about me without having to explain them, without talking—although Nina does plenty of that.

I look around the table, at the inconspicuous, relaxed faces of my family members, and it hits me that, at last, I have to try very hard to remember why I came back here in the first place. The lingering despair—that ever-present tightening in my chest—has made way for something else. Dr. Hakim would urge me to try to put it into words, but he's not here, so I don't need to try to articulate that simmering feeling of possibility, the gratitude for the long moments of peace and quiet in my mind I can now enjoy, the waking up without immense dread for a new day, the realization that life, after all, can be largely okay.

I love you. I don't say it out loud—The Goodmans will never be a family of I-love-yous—but thinking it is more than enough.

———

"A sock, huh?" Kay asks while we're getting ready for bed.

"Don't you start."

"I feel your pain, honey. Socks are so inadequate." She sits on the edge of the bed and motions for me to perch next to her. "Come here."

Kay never has to tell me twice, so I hurry to her side. Once I'm seated, she leans toward the bedside table and takes out a box.

"Going away gift," she says, as she hands it to me.

"Oh." I pull my lips into a pout. "But I didn't get you anything."

"You're coming back, Ella. That's the only present I'll ever need." She nods at the box. "Go on. Open it."

I tear at the wrapping paper and unearth a plastic box with a see-through front. My eyes widen when my brain registers what's inside: a quite sizable pink dildo, flanked by a black strap-on harness.

Amazed, I look at Kay. "What the hell am I going to do with that in Boston?"

"Read the card." Her eyes have gone wildly dark again, like they do before we fuck. I find a white envelope taped to the back of the box. I open it and the front of the card shows a sad-faced cartoon figure with tears in its eyes, saying, "So sad you're going away."

My heart breaks a little at the sight of it, and I start dreading the moment Kay will drop me at the airport tomorrow—the moment we'll have to say goodbye, at least for a few months.

I open the card and read what she wrote: 'I think I'll go with you.' A folded sheet of A4 paper is nestled inside the card and when I unfold it I see it's a plane ticket to Boston with Kay's name on it.

"For real?" Misty-eyed, I look at her.

"Of course." She scoots closer. "I want to be with you when you walk back into your house. I don't want you to do that alone."

I'm so flabbergasted, it takes a few seconds for the meaning of her words to sink in.

"I love you," I say. Out loud, this time.

ACKNOWLEDGMENTS

Caroline, for always reading first, and being my rock.

Maria, for giving me a new set of lenses to see myself through (and being the sort of beta-reader any writer dreams of).

Cheyenne, for helping me shape all my emotions into relatable, grammatically correct sentences.

My sister, for the endless chuckles (even when I don't feel like laughing).

My parents, for not needing me to say I'm sorry.

Thank you.

MESSAGE FROM THE AUTHOR

Dear Reader,

Even though At the Water's Edge is fiction, writing this book has been a very emotional journey for me. I have literally cried my way through it, expelling many a demon in the process. It only took me fifteen years. I can't thank you enough for reading this story that holds so much importance to me.

The subject matter of At the Water's Edge is no joke and if reading it has affected you in any way and/or left you needing to talk, you can find information about suicide prevention centers across the world at this link:

https://www.iasp.info/resources/Crisis_Centres/

I won't end this note with an empty phrase like 'You are not alone', but, if you're looking for an example of someone who has made it through to the other end of depression—with lots of ups and downs—that person is addressing you right now. It's not impossible.

Love,

Harper

ABOUT THE AUTHOR

Harper Bliss is a best-selling lesbian romance author. Among her most-loved books are the highly dramatic French Kissing and the often thought-provoking Pink Bean series.

Harper lived in Hong Kong for 7 years, travelled the world for a bit, and has now settled in Brussels (Belgium) with her wife and photogenic cat, Dolly Purrton.

Together with her wife, she hosts a weekly podcast called Harper Bliss & Her Mrs.

Harper loves hearing from readers and you can reach her at the email address below.

www.harperbliss.com
harper@harperbliss.com

Printed in Great Britain
by Amazon

60689716R00139